A GAME OF THRONES

THE GRAPHIC NOVEL

VOLUME 4

GEORGE R. R.
MARTIN

A GAME OF THRONES

THE GRAPHIC NOVEL

VOLUME 4

ADAPTED BY DANIEL ABRAHAM

ART BY TOMMY PATTERSON

COLORS BY SANDRA MOLINA AND IVAN NUNES

LETTERING BY MARSHALL DILLON

ORIGINAL SERIES COVER ART BY

MIKE S. MILLER

Published in Great Britain by Harper*Voyager*, an imprint of HarperCollins*Publishers* 2015

ISBN 978-0-00-813220-0

Printed in China.

www.harpervoyagerbooks.co.uk

9 8 7 6 5 4 3 2

Graphic novel interior design by Foltz Design.

Visit us online at www.DYNAMITE.com
Follow us on Twitter @dynamitecomics
Like us on Facebook /Dynamitecomics
Watch us on YouTube /Dynamitecomics
On Tumblr dynamitecomics.tumblr.com

CONTENTS

ISSUE #19
PAGE 2

ISSUE #20
PAGE 32

ISSUE #21
PAGE 62

ISSUE #22
PAGE 92

ISSUE #23
PAGE 122

ISSUE #24
PAGE 152

THE MAKING OF
A GAME OF THRONES: THE GRAPHIC NOVEL: VOLUME 4
PAGE 183

A GAME OF THRONES

THE GRAPHIC NOVEL

VOLUME 4

ISSUE #19

BY THEIR FIRES, I CALL THEM TWENTY THOUSAND STRONG.
YOUR FATHER?
OR MY BROTHER JAIME. WE SHALL KNOW SOON ENOUGH.

IT MIGHT BE BEST IF I RODE DOWN ALONE.

SHAGGA SON OF DOLF LIKES THIS NOT.
SHAGGA WILL GO WITH THE BOYMAN. IF THE BOYMAN LIES, SHAGGA WILL CHOP OFF HIS MANHOOD –

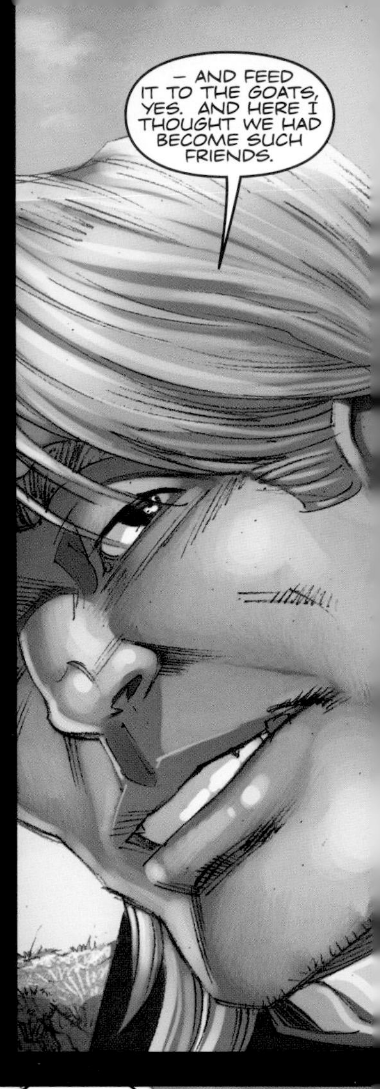
– AND FEED IT TO THE GOATS, YES. AND HERE I THOUGHT WE HAD BECOME SUCH FRIENDS.

AS YOU WILL. SHAGGA WILL RIDE WITH ME, AND CHELLA FOR THE BLACK EARS.

CONN FOR THE STONE CROWS, ULF FOR THE MOON BROTHERS, AND TIMETT SON OF TIMETT FOR THE BURNED MEN.
THE REST WILL STAY BEHIND. TRY NOT TO KILL AND MAIM EACH OTHER WHILE I'M GONE.

THEY PASSED BLACKENED FIELDS AND BURNED HOLDFASTS. TYRION SAW NO BODIES, BUT THE AIR WAS FULL OF CARRION CROWS.

SER FLEMMENT!

TYRION! WE FEARED YOU DEAD. THESE... COMPANIONS OF YOURS...
BOSOM FRIENDS AND LOYAL RETAINERS. WHERE WILL I FIND MY LORD FATHER?
HE HAS TAKEN THE INN AT THE CROSSROADS FOR HIS QUARTERS.

A ROOM, A MEAL, AND A FLAGON OF WINE. THAT WAS ALL I ASKED.

THE LAD WON'T STEAL YOUR MARE, SHAGGA. IF HE DOES, CHOP OFF HIS MANHOOD AND FEED IT TO THE GOATS.
IF YOU CAN FIND ANY.

MY MEN WANT MEAT AND MEAD. SEE THAT THEY GET IT. AND WHERE IS MY FATHER?
IN THE COMMON ROOM WITH LORD KEVAN, M'LORD.

TYRION!
UNCLE.
MY LORD FATHER. WHAT A PLEASURE IT IS TO FIND YOU HERE.
I SEE THAT RUMORS OF YOUR DEMISE WERE UNFOUNDED.
SORRY TO DISAPPOINT YOU.
NO NEED TO LEAP UP AND EMBRACE ME. I WOULDN'T WANT YOU TO STRAIN YOURSELF.

KIND OF YOU TO GO TO WAR FOR ME.
BY MY LIGHTS, IT WAS YOU WHO STARTED THIS. YOUR BROTHER WOULD NEVER HAVE SUBMITTED TO CAPTURE AT THE HANDS OF A WOMAN.
THAT'S ONE WAY WE DIFFER, JAIME AND I. HE'S TALLER AS WELL.
I HAD NO CHOICE BUT TO RIDE. NO MAN SHEDS LANNISTER BLOOD WITH IMPUNITY.
HEAR ME ROAR.
AND NONE OF MY BLOOD WAS ACTUALLY SHED. MORREC AND JYCK WERE KILLED, THOUGH.
I SUPPOSE YOU WILL WANT NEW MEN.
DON'T TROUBLE YOURSELF. I'VE ACQUIRED SOME OF MY OWN.
HOW IS YOUR WAR GOING?

WELL ENOUGH, FOR THE NONCE. SER EDMURE TULLY HAD SCATTERED SMALL TROOPS TO STOP OUR RAIDING, BUT WE WERE ABLE TO DESTROY MOST PIECEMEAL BEFORE THEY REGROUPED.

YOUR BROTHER HAS BEEN COVERING HIMSELF IN GLORY. HE SMASHED LORDS VANCE AND PIPER, AND MET THE MASSED POWER OF THE TULLYS UNDER THE WALLS OF RIVERRUN.
YOUR FATHER AND I HAVE ALSO DONE OUR PARTS. RAVENWOOD FELL, AND HARRENHAL YIELDED FOR WANT OF MEN TO DEFEND IT.
THE LORDS OF THE TRIDENT HAVE BEEN PUT TO ROUT.
LEAVING YOU UNOPPOSED?
NOT WHOLLY. THE MALLISTERS HOLD SEAGARD, AND WALDER FREY IS MARSHALING HIS FORCES AT THE TWINS.
ONCE JAIME TAKES RIVERRUN, THEY WILL BOTH BEND THE KNEE. UNLESS THE STARKS AND THE ARRYNS COME FORTH TO OPPOSE US, THIS WAR IS AS GOOD AS WON.

I WOULD NOT FRET ABOUT THE ARRYNS AS MUCH AS THE STARKS. LORD EDDARD –
– IS OUR HOSTAGE. HIS SON HAS CALLED THE BANNERS AND HAS GATHERED A STRONG HOST AROUND HIM, BUT HE'S A CHILD.

AND HOW HAS MY LOVELY SISTER GOTTEN ROBERT TO IMPRISON HIS DEAR FRIEND NED?
ROBERT BARATHEON IS DEAD AND YOUR NEPHEW RULES IN KING'S LANDING.

MY SISTER, YOU MEAN.
THAT DID TAKE HIM ABACK. THE REALM WOULD BE MUCH DIFFERENT WITH CERSEI RULING IT.

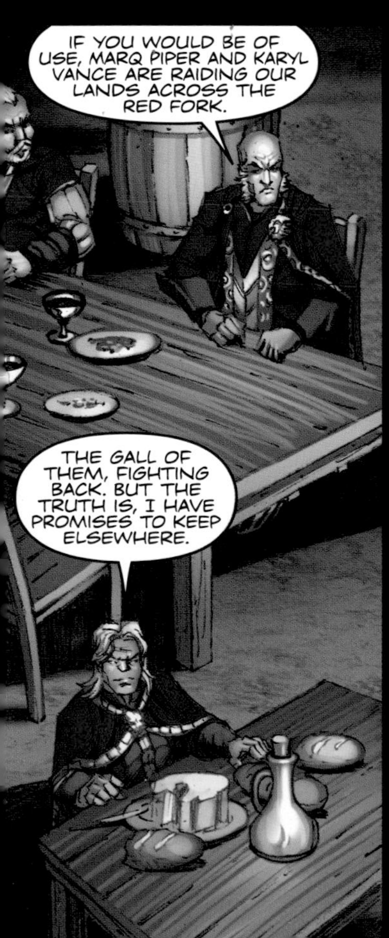
IF YOU WOULD BE OF USE, MARQ PIPER AND KARYL VANCE ARE RAIDING OUR LANDS ACROSS THE RED FORK.
THE GALL OF THEM, FIGHTING BACK. BUT THE TRUTH IS, I HAVE PROMISES TO KEEP ELSEWHERE.

I SHALL REQUIRE THREE THOUSAND HELMS, AND AS MANY HAUBERKS. PLUS SWORDS, PIKES, STEEL SPEARHEADS, BREASTPLATES, GAUNTLETS –

CRASH

LITTLE REDCAPE!
WHEN NEXT YOU BARE STEEL ON SHAGGA SON OF DOLF, I WILL CHOP OFF YOUR MANHOOD AND ROAST IT ON THE FIRE!
WHAT?
NO GOATS?
AND WHO MIGHT YOU BE?
THEY FOLLOWED ME HOME, FATHER.
MAY I KEEP THEM?
THEY DON'T EAT MUCH.
BY WHAT RIGHT DO YOU SAVAGES INTRUDE ON OUR COUNCIL!
SAVAGES, LOWLANDER? WE ARE FREE MEN, AND FREE MEN SIT ON ALL WAR COUNCILS!
TYRION, HAVE YOU HAVE FORGOTTEN YOUR COURTESIES? KINDLY ACQUAINT US WITH OUR HONORED GUESTS.

WITH PLEASURE. THE FAIR MAID IS CHELLA DAUGHTER OF CHEYK OF THE BLACK EARS.

I'M NO MAID. MY SONS HAVE TAKEN FIFTY EARS AMONG THEM!
MAY THEY TAKE FIFTY MORE.

SHAGGA SON OF DOLF IS THE ONE WHO LOOKS LIKE CASTERLY ROCK WITH HAIR.
CONN AND SHAGGA ARE OF THE STONE CROWS. ULF IS OF THE MOON BROTHERS. TIMETT, THE BURNED MEN.

AND THIS IS BRONN, A SELLSWORD OF NO PARTICULAR ALLEGIANCE.
HE HAS ALREADY CHANGED SIDES TWICE IN THE SHORT TIME I'VE KNOWN HIM.

YOU AND HE OUGHT TO GET ON FAMOUSLY, FATHER.

EVEN IN THE WEST, WE KNOW OF THE PROWESS OF THE WARRIOR CLANS. WHAT BRINGS YOU DOWN FROM YOUR STRONGHOLDS, MY LORDS?
HORSES?
THE BOYMAN'S PROMISE OF SILK AND STEEL.
MY LORD TYWIN!

MY LORD! SER ADDAM BID ME TELL YOU THE STARK HOST IS MOVING DOWN THE CAUSEWAY.
SPLENDID. TELL HIM TO FALL BACK, HARASS THEIR FLANKS, AND DRAW THEM SOUTH.

RIDE WITH ME AGAINST MY ENEMIES, AND YOU SHALL HAVE ALL MY SON PROMISED AND MORE.
WHY SHOULD WE NEED THE FATHER'S PROMISE WHEN WE HAVE THE SON'S?
I SAID NOTHING OF ***NEED***. YOU NEED DO NOTHING.
THE MEN OF THE WINTERLANDS ARE MEN OF IRON AND ICE. EVEN MY BOLDEST KNIGHTS FEAR TO FACE THEM.

THE BURNED MEN FEAR NOTHING! TIMETT WILL RIDE WITH THE LIONS.
WHERE THE BURNED MEN GO, THE STONE CROWS HAVE BEEN THERE FIRST.
SHAGGA SON OF DOLF WILL CUT OFF THEIR MANHOODS AND FEED THEM TO THE CROWS!
WE RIDE WITH YOU, LION LORD, BUT ONLY IF YOUR HALFMAN SON GOES WITH US.
UNTIL WE HOLD THE STEEL HE PLEDGES, HIS LIFE IS OURS.

JOY.

AS ROBB'S HOST TROOPED DOWN THE CAUSEWAY THROUGH THE BLACK BOGS OF THE NECK AND THE RIVERLANDS BEYOND, CATELYN'S APPREHENSIONS GREW.
HER DAYS WERE ANXIOUS AND HER NIGHTS RESTLESS. EVERY RAVEN THAT FLEW OVERHEAD MADE HER TEETH CLENCH.
ROBB RODE AT THE FRONT OF THE COLUMN. EACH DAY HE HAD ONE OF HIS GREAT LORDS RIDE WITH HIM, HONORING EACH MAN IN TURN, SHOWING NO FAVORITES.
HE HAD LEARNED SO MUCH FROM NED, BUT WAS IT **ENOUGH?**

THE BLACKFISH HAD TAKEN A HUNDRED MEN AND HORSES AND RACED AHEAD TO SCREEN THEIR MOVEMENTS AND SCOUT THE WAY. BUT THE REPORTS SER BRYNDEN'S RIDERS BROUGHT BACK DID LITTLE REASSURE HER.
IT WAS NEAR MIDDAY WHEN THEIR VANGUARD CAME IN SIGHT OF THE TWINS, WHERE THE LORDS OF THE CROSSING HAD THEIR SEAT.
WALDER FREY, LORD OF THE CROSSING, HAD ASSEMBLED A FORCE OF NEAR FOUR THOUSAND MEN AT HIS TWIN CASTLES ON THE GREEN FORK.

LORD FREY SHOULD HAVE SENT HIS MEN TO RIVERRUN WHEN LORD EDMURE CALLED THE BANNERS, YET HERE THEY REMAIN.
EVEN WITH FOUR THOUSAND MEN, HE CANNOT HOPE TO FIGHT THE LANNISTERS BY HIMSELF. SURELY HE MEANS TO JOIN HIS POWER TO OURS.
DOES HE? I WONDER.
EXPECT NOTHING OF WALDER FREY, AND YOU WILL NEVER BE SURPRISED.
BUT HE'S YOUR FATHER'S BANNERMAN!
SOME MEN TAKE THEIR OATHS MORE SERIOUSLY THAN OTHERS, ROBB. AND LORD WALDER WAS ALWAYS FRIENDLIER WITH CASTERLY ROCK THAN MY FATHER WOULD HAVE LIKED.
ONE OF HIS SONS IS MARRIED TO TYWIN LANNISTER'S SISTER.
STILL, LORD WALDER HAS SIRED A GREAT MANY CHILDREN OVER THE YEARS, AND THEY MUST MARRY SOMEONE...
YOU THINK HE MEANS TO BETRAY US?
I DOUBT EVEN LORD FREY KNOWS WHAT LORD FREY INTENDS TO DO. HE HAS AN OLD MAN'S CAUTION, A YOUNG MAN'S AMBITION, AND HAS NEVER LACKED CUNNING.

THE RIVER'S RUNNING HIGH AND FAST. SER BRYNDEN SAYS IT CAN'T BE FORDED. NOT THIS FAR NORTH.
YOU HAVE FIVE TIMES HIS NUMBERS. YOU CAN TAKE THE TWINS BY FORCE.
I **MUST** HAVE THAT CROSSING.
NOT EASILY, AND NOT IN TIME. WHILE YOU MOUNTED A SIEGE, TYWIN LANNISTER'S HOST WOULD ASSAULT FROM THE REAR.
WHAT WOULD MY LORD FATHER DO?
FIND A WAY ACROSS. WHATEVER IT TOOK.

THE NEXT MORNING, BRYNDEN TULLY RODE BACK HIMSELF. THE NEWS WAS BAD. A BATTLE AT RIVERRUN, EDMURE TAKEN PRISONER, AND THE SURVIVORS UNDER SIEGE BY JAIME LANNISTER.
LORD FREY, IN THE MEANTIME, HAD PULLED HIS FORCES INSIDE HIS CASTLES AND BARRED HIS GATES.

DAMN THE MAN! I'LL PULL THE PULL THE TWINS DOWN AROUND HIS EARS IF I HAVE TO.
YOU SOUND LIKE A SULKY BOY.

THE FREYS HAVE HELD THIS CROSSING FOR SIX HUNDRED YEARS, ROBB, AND THEY HAVE NEVER FAILED TO EXACT THEIR TOLL.

WHAT TOLL? WHAT DOES HE WANT?
THAT IS WHAT WE MUST DISCOVER.

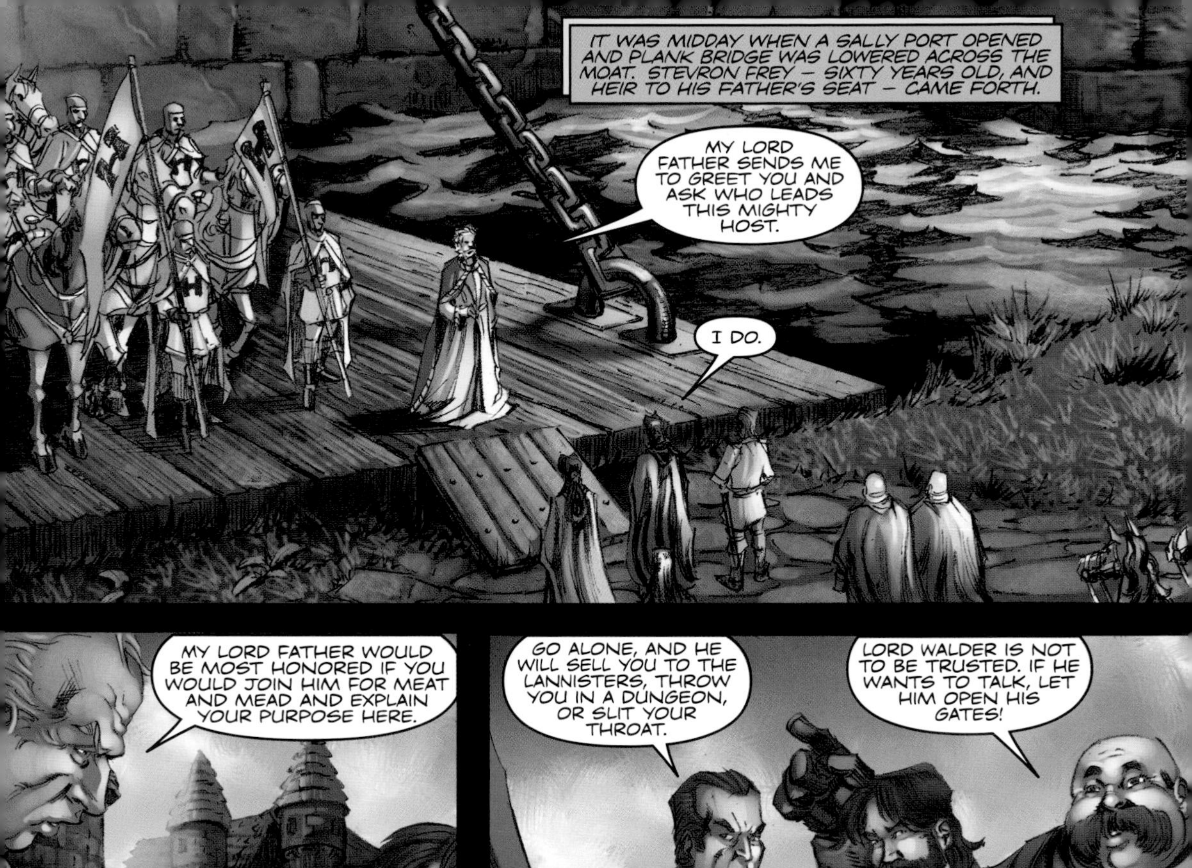
IT WAS MIDDAY WHEN A SALLY PORT OPENED AND PLANK BRIDGE WAS LOWERED ACROSS THE MOAT. STEVRON FREY — SIXTY YEARS OLD, AND HEIR TO HIS FATHER'S SEAT — CAME FORTH.
MY LORD FATHER SENDS ME TO GREET YOU AND ASK WHO LEADS THIS MIGHTY HOST.
I DO.

MY LORD FATHER WOULD BE MOST HONORED IF YOU WOULD JOIN HIM FOR MEAT AND MEAD AND EXPLAIN YOUR PURPOSE HERE.

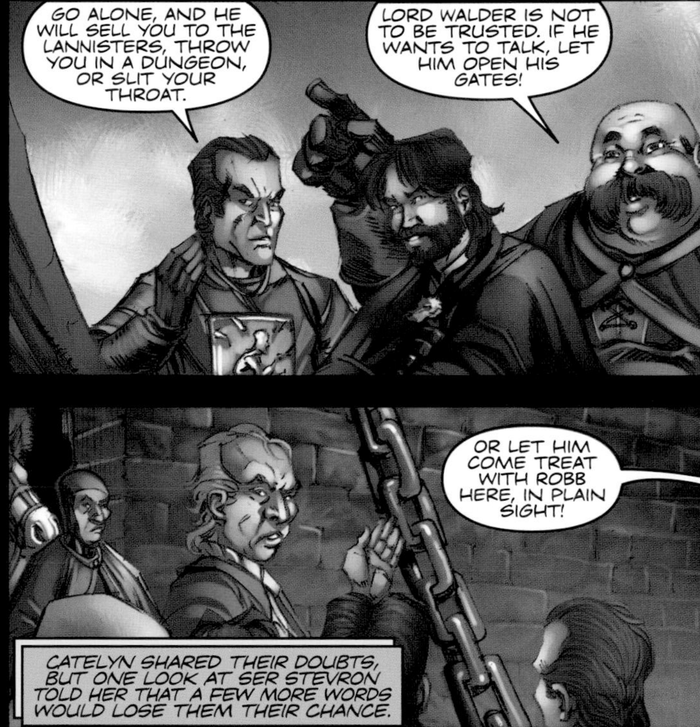
GO ALONE, AND HE WILL SELL YOU TO THE LANNISTERS, THROW YOU IN A DUNGEON, OR SLIT YOUR THROAT.
LORD WALDER IS NOT TO BE TRUSTED. IF HE WANTS TO TALK, LET HIM OPEN HIS GATES!
OR LET HIM COME TREAT WITH ROBB HERE, IN PLAIN SIGHT!
CATELYN SHARED THEIR DOUBTS, BUT ONE LOOK AT SER STEVRON TOLD HER THAT A FEW MORE WORDS WOULD LOSE THEM THEIR CHANCE.

I WILL GO.
I HAVE KNOWN LORD WALDER SINCE I WAS A GIRL. HE WOULD NEVER OFFER ME ANY HARM.
UNLESS HE SAW SOME PROFIT IN IT, SHE ADDED SILENTLY.

CATELYN'S FATHER ONCE SAID THAT WALDER FREY COULD FIELD AN ARMY OUT OF HIS BREECHES. THE GREAT HALL HELD HIS TWENTY-ONE SONS, PLUS THIRTY-SIX GRANDSONS, NINETEEN GREAT-GRANDSONS, AND NUMEROUS DAUGHTERS, GRANDDAUGHTERS, BASTARDS AND GRANDBASTARDS.
HE WAS NINETY. HIS LATEST WIFE WAS A FRAIL THING OF SIXTEEN.

IT IS A GREAT PLEASURE TO SEE YOU AGAIN, MY LORD.
I DOUBT THAT. SPARE ME YOUR SWEET WORDS, LADY CATELYN. I AM TOO OLD.

IS YOUR BOY TOO PROUD TO COME BEFORE ME HIMSELF? WHAT AM I TO DO WITH **YOU?**

FATHER, YOU FORGET YOURSELF. LADY STARK IS HERE AT YOUR INVITATION.
DID I ASK YOU? YOU ARE NOT LORD FREY UNTIL I **DIE**. DO I LOOK **DEAD?**

WELCOME, HONORED GUEST, TO MY HALL.
THERE. NOW THAT I'VE OBSERVED THE COURTESIES, WHY **ARE** YOU HERE?

TO ASK THAT YOU OPEN YOUR GATES. MY SON AND HIS BANNERMEN ARE ANXIOUS TO CROSS THE RIVER AND BE ON THEIR WAY.
TO RIVERRUN?

TO RIVERRUN — WHERE I MIGHT HAVE EXPECTED TO FIND YOU, MY LORD.
ARE YOU NOT MY FATHER'S BANNERMAN?

I CALLED MY SWORDS. IS IT MY FAULT YOUR FOOL BROTHER LOST HIS BATTLE BEFORE WE COULD MARCH?

ALL THE MORE REASON WE MUST GO QUICKLY. WHERE CAN WE GO TO TALK, MY LORD?
WE'RE TALKING NOW.

WELL, WHAT ARE YOU ALL LOOKING AT? GET OUT! LADY STARK WANTS TO SPEAK WITH ME IN PRIVATE.
MIGHT BE SHE HAS DESIGNS ON MY FIDELITY. *HEH.* OUT, OUT, ***OUT!***

THEY'RE ALL WAITING FOR ME TO DIE, BUT I KEEP DISAPPOINTING THEM.
I HAVE EVERY HOPE THAT YOU WILL LIVE TO BE A HUNDRED.
THAT WOULD BOIL THEM, TO BE SURE. NOW. WHAT DO YOU WANT TO SAY?
WE WANT TO CROSS.
THAT'S BLUNT. WHY SHOULD I LET YOU?
"IF YOU WERE STRONG ENOUGH TO CLIMB YOUR OWN BATTLEMENTS, YOU WOULD SEE THAT MY SON HAS TWENTY THOUSAND MEN OUTSIDE YOUR WALLS."
DON'T TRY TO FRIGHTEN ME, MY LADY.
YOUR HUSBAND IS IN A TRAITOR'S CELL UNDER THE RED KEEP, YOUR FATHER IS DYING, AND JAIME LANNISTER'S GOT YOUR BROTHER IN CHAINS.
WHAT SHOULD I FEAR? THAT SON OF YOURS?
I'LL MATCH YOU SON FOR SON, AND STILL HAVE EIGHTEEN WHEN YOURS ARE ALL DEAD.

YOU SWORE AN OATH TO MY FATHER.

I SAID SOME WORDS...BUT I SWORE OATHS TO THE CROWN, TOO, I SEEMS TO ME.
JOFFREY'S THE KING NOW. AND IF I HAD THE SENSE THE GODS GAVE A FISH, I'D HELP THE LANNISTERS TO BOIL YOU ALL.

THEN WHY DON'T YOU?

"LORD TYWIN LANNISTER, THE PROUD AND SPLENDID. WHAT A GREAT MAN THAT ONE IS, WITH HIS GOLD AND HIS LIONS."
"I WAGER HE BREAKS WIND JUST LIKE ME, BUT YOU'LL NEVER HEAR HIM ADMIT IT."

AND WHAT'S HE GOT TO BE SO PUFFED UP ABOUT? ONLY TWO SONS, AND ONE'S A TWISTED LITTLE MONSTER.
I'LL MATCH HIM SON FOR SON, AND STILL HAVE NINETEEN AND A HALF LEFT WHEN ALL OF HIS ARE DEAD!

IF LORD TYWIN WANTS MY HELP, HE CAN BLOODY WELL ASK FOR IT!

THAT WAS ALL CATELYN NEEDED TO HEAR.
I AM ASKING FOR YOUR HELP, MY LORD. AND MY FATHER AND MY BROTHER AND MY LORD HUSBAND AND MY SONS ARE ASKING WITH MY VOICE.
SAVE YOUR SWEET WORDS, MY LADY. SWEET WORDS I GET FROM MY WIFE.
DID YOU SEE HER? SIXTEEN SHE IS, AND I'D WAGER SHE GIVES ME A SON BY THIS TIME NEXT YEAR.

OR A DAUGHTER; THAT CAN'T BE HELPED. AND LIKE AS NOT, SHE'LL WANT TO NAME IT WALDER OR WALDA.
THEY ALL DO, SO I'LL FAVOR THEM.

BUT YOUR LORD FATHER DIDN'T COME TO MY WEDDING. AND HE WOULDN'T MARRY MY DAUGHTER TO HIS EDMURE. AN INSULT I CALL IT.

AND YOUR LADY SISTER? SHE'S FULL AS BAD.
WHEN I PROPOSED THAT LORD ARRYN FOSTER TWO OF MY GRANDSONS AND SEND HIS SON TO THE TWINS, SHE FROSTED UP AS IF I'D SUGGESTED MAKING A EUNUCH OF THE BOY!
AND WHEN LORD ARRYN SAID HIS CHILD WAS GOING TO DRAGONSTONE TO FOSTER WITH STANNIS BARATHEON, SHE STORMED OFF WITHOUT A WORD OF REGRETS.
ALL THE HAND COULD GIVE ME WAS APOLOGIES. AND WHAT GOOD ARE APOLOGIES?
BUT I'D UNDERSTOOD LYSA'S BOY WAS DO FOSTER WITH LORD TYWIN...
DO YOU THINK I CAN'T TELL LORD STANNIS FROM LORD TYWIN? THEY'RE BOTH BUNGHOLES WHO THINK THEY'RE TOO NOBLE TO SHIT, BUT I KNOW THE DIFFERENCE!
ONLY JON ARRYN DIED, SO WHAT DOES IT MATTER?

YOU SAY YOU WANT TO CROSS THE RIVER?
WE DO.
WELL YOU CAN'T. NOT UNLESS I ALLOW IT, AND WHY **SHOULD** I?
THE REST WAS ONLY HAGGLING.

IT'S DONE. LORD WALDER WILL GRANT YOU MEANS OF CROSSING AND HIS SWORDS, LESS THE FOUR HUNDRED HE NEEDS TO HOLD THE TWINS.
I SUGGEST YOU ALSO LEAVE FOUR HUNDRED OF YOUR OWN...BUT MAKE CERTAIN YOU GIVE THE COMMAND TO A MAN YOU CAN TRUST.
LORD WALDER MAY NEED HELP KEEPING FAITH.
AS YOU SAY. SER HELMAN TALLHEART, DO YOU THINK?
A FINE CHOICE.
SO... WHAT DID HE WANT FROM US?
I HAVE AGREED TO TAKE TWO OF HIS GRANDSONS AS WARDS. BRAN SHOULD WELCOME THE COMPANIONSHIP OF LADS NEAR HIS OWN AGE.
THEY ARE BOTH NAMED WALDER, IT WOULD SEEM.

LORD FREY'S SON OLYVAR IS TO SERVE AS YOUR PERSONAL SQUIRE, AND BE KNIGHTED EVENTUALLY.
ALSO, IF ARYA IS RETURNED TO US SAFELY, IT IS AGREED SHE WILL MARRY LORD WALDER'S YOUNGEST SON WHEN THEY BOTH COME OF AGE.
SHE WON'T LIKE THAT ONE BIT.
AND *YOU* ARE TO WED ONE OF HIS DAUGHTERS WHEN THE FIGHTING IS DONE.
HIS LORDSHIP HAS GRACIOUSLY CONSENTED TO ALLOW YOU TO CHOOSE WHICHEVER GIRL YOU PREFER. THERE ARE A NUMBER THAT MIGHT BE SUITABLE.
CAN I REFUSE?
NOT IF YOU WISH TO CROSS.

THEN I CONSENT.
THEY CROSSED AT EVENFALL. THE LARGER PART OF THE NORTHERN HOST REMAINED ON THE EAST BANK UNDER THE COMMAND OF ROOSE BOLTON, AND STILL IT TOOK THEM HOURS TO CROSS.
BOLTON WOULD MARCH SOUTH TO CONFRONT LORD TYWIN'S HUGE FORCE. ROBB WOULD TAKE THE REST TO RIVERRUN.
FOR GOOD OR ILL, HER SON HAD THROWN THE DICE.

ISSUE #20

WHEN THE BATTLE WAS DONE, DANY RODE THROUGH THE FIELDS OF THE DEAD.
DYING HORSES LIFTED THEIR HEADS AND SCREAMED AS SHE PASSED. WOUNDED MEN MOANED AND PRAYED.
DOTHRAKI HOOVES HAD TORN THE EARTH AND TRAMPLED THE RYE AND LENTILS. ARAKHS AND ARROWS HAD SOWN A TERRIBLE NEW CROP AND WATERED IT WITH BLOOD.

MERCY MEN TOOK HEADS FROM THE DEAD AND DYING ALIKE. AFTER THEM WOULD COME A FLOCK OF SMALL GIRLS PULLING ARROWS FROM THE CORPSES TO FILL THEIR BASKETS.
AND LAST OF ALL, THE DOGS.
THE SHEEP HAD BEEN DEAD THE LONGEST. KHAL OGO'S RIDERS HAD KILLED THEM. NO MAN OF DROGO'S KHALASAR WOULD WASTE ARROWS ON SHEEP WHEN THERE WERE SHEPHERDS YET TO KILL.
THE WOMEN AND CHILDREN OF OGO'S KHALASAR WALKED WITH SULLEN PRIDE EVEN IN DEFEAT AND BONDAGE. THEY WERE SLAVES NOW, BUT SEEMED NOT TO FEAR IT.
IT WAS DIFFERENT FOR THE TOWNSFOLK.
MOTHERS STUMBLED ALONG WITH DEAD FACES, PULLING SOBBING CHILDREN BEHIND. THE DOTHRAKI CALLED THEM THE LAMB MEN, AND DANY PITIED THEM. SHE REMEMBERED WHAT TERROR FELT LIKE.

THEY WERE HERDERS OF SHEEP AND EATERS OF VEGETABLES, AND KHAL DROGO SAID THEY BELONGED SOUTH OF THE RIVER BEND.
THE GRASS OF THE DOTHRAKI SEA WAS NOT MEANT FOR SHEEP.

THE DOTHRAKI HAD MOCKED SER JORAH'S ARMOR, BUT THE KNIGHT HAD SPIT THE INSULTS BACK, AND THE RIDER WHOSE TAUNTS HAD BEEN LOUDEST HAD BEEN LEFT TO BLEED TO DEATH.
YOUR LORD HUSBAND AWAITS YOU WITHIN THE TOWN.
DROGO TOOK NO HARM?

A FEW CUTS. NOTHING OF CONSEQUENCE.

HE SLEW TWO KHALS TODAY. KHAL OGO FIRST, AND THEN THE SON, FOGO, WHO BECAME KHAL WHEN OGO DIED.
OGO AND HIS SON HAD SHARED THE HIGH BENCH WITH HER LORD HUSBAND AT THE NAMING FEAST IN VAES DOTHRAK, WHERE ALL QUARRELS WERE PUT ASIDE.

IT WAS DIFFERENT IN THE GRASS. OGO'S KHALASAR HAD BEEN ATTACKING THE TOWN WHEN KHAL DROGO CAUGHT HIM.
SHE WONDERED WHAT THE LAMB MEN HAD THOUGHT WHEN THEY FIRST SAW THE DUST OF HER HUSBAND'S HORSES, AND WHETHER THEY HAD MISTAKEN IT FOR DELIVERANCE.

THIS WAS THE DELIVERANCE THE DOTHRAKI BROUGHT THE LAMB MEN.
AAAIEEE!
MOST OF OGO'S RIDERS FLED.
THERE MAY BE AS MANY AS TEN THOUSAND CAPTIVES.
TEN THOUSAND SLAVES. DANY WANTED TO CRY, BUT SHE WAS THE BLOOD OF THE DRAGON.

THIS IS WHAT WAR LOOKS LIKE. THIS IS THE PRICE OF THE IRON THRONE.
I'VE TOLD THE KHAL HE OUGHT TO MAKE FOR MEEREEN. THEY'LL PAY A BETTER PRICE THAN A SLAVING CARAVAN.
AH AH AIEEE!
THEY HAD A PLAGUE LAST YEAR, AND THE BROTHELS ARE PAYING DOUBLE FOR YOUNG GIRLS, AND TRIPLE FOR BOYS UNDER TEN–

--EEE...
MAKE THEM STOP!

KHALEESI?
YOU HEARD MY WORDS.

JHOGO. QUARO. YOU WILL AID SER JORAH.
I WANT NO RAPE.

PRINCESS, YOU HAVE A GENTLE HEART, BUT THIS IS HOW IT HAS ALWAYS BEEN. THOSE MEN SHED BLOOD FOR THE KHAL.
NOW THEY CLAIM THEIR REWARD.

SHE IS NOTHING, KHALEESI. THE RIDERS DO HER HONOR.

IF HER WAILING OFFENDS YOUR EARS, JHOGO WILL BRING YOU HER TONGUE.
I WILL NOT HAVE HER HARMED!

I CLAIM HER.
DO AS I COMMEND YOU, OR KHAL DROGO WILL KNOW THE REASON WHY.
AI, KHALEESI.
GO WITH THEM.
AS YOU COMMAND.

YOU ARE YOUR BROTHER'S SISTER IN TRUTH.

VISERYS?
NO. RHAEGAR.

JHOGO SHOUTED, AND THE RAPERS LAUGHED AT HIM.

BUT THE LAUGHTER QUICKLY TURNED TO CURSES. THE RIDERS LOOKED ACROSS THE ROAD TO HER WITH COLD, BLACK EYES.

THE MAN ATOP THE LAMB GIRL SEEMED UNAWARE OF WHAT WAS GOING ON AROUND HIM UNTIL SER JORAH WRENCHED HIM AWAY.
THE FIGHT THAT CAME AFTER WAS BRIEF.

WHAT DO YOU WANT DONE WITH HER?

DOREAH, SEE TO HER HURTS. YOU DO NOT HAVE A RIDER'S LOOK. PERHAPS SHE WILL NOT FEAR YOU.
THE REST, WITH ME.

IT WAS WORSE WITHIN THE TOWN. MANY OF THE HOUSES WERE AFIRE. HEADLESS CORPSES FILLED THE NARROW, TWISTY LANES.
THEY PASSED OTHER WOMEN BEING RAPED. EACH TIME, DANY MADE AN END OF IT AND CLAIMED THE VICTIM AS A SLAVE.
ONE OF THEM BLESSED DANY HALTINGLY IN THE COMMON TONGUE. FROM OTHERS SHE GOT ONLY FLAT BLACK STARES.
THEY WERE AFRAID SHE HAD SAVED THEM FOR SOME WORSE FATE.

YOU CANNOT CLAIM THEM ALL, CHILD.
I AM KHALEESI, HEIR TO THE SEVEN KINGDOMS, THE BLOOD OF THE DRAGON.
IT IS NOT FOR YOU TO TELL ME WHAT I CANNOT DO.

THEY FOUND KHAL DROGO BEFORE THE TEMPLE.
MY SUN-AND-STARS IS WOUNDED!

IS SCRATCH FROM ONE BLOODRIDER TO KHAL OGO. I KILL HIM FOR IT, AND OGO TOO.

NO MAN CAN STAND BEFORE THE FATHER OF THE STALLION WHO MOUNTS THE WORLD.
QOTHO! KHAL DROGO!

THE WARRIOR SPOKE TO QOTHO IN A STREAM OF ANGRY DOTHRAKI TOO FAST FOR HER TO UNDERSTAND.

THIS ONE IS MAGO WHO RIDES IN THE KHAS OF KO JHAQO. HE SAYS THE KHALEESI HAS TAKEN HIS SPOILS.

A DAUGHTER OF THE LAMB THAT WAS HIS TO MOUNT.

IT PLEASES ME TO HOLD THEM SAFE.
IF YOUR WARRIORS WOULD MOUNT THESE WOMEN, LET THEM TAKE THEM GENTLY AND KEEP THEM AS WIVES.

DOES THE HORSE BREED WITH THE SHEEP?
THE **DRAGON** FEEDS ON HORSE AND SHEEP ALIKE!

YOU SEE HOW FIERCE SHE GROWS? IT IS MY SON INSIDE HER, FILLING HER WITH FIRE.

RIDE SLOWLY, QOTHO. IF THE MOTHER DOES NOT BURN YOU, THE SON WILL TRAMPLE YOU INTO THE MUD.

AND YOU, MAGO! HOLD YOUR TONGUE AND FIND ANOTHER LAMB TO MOUNT. THESE BELONG TO MY KHALEESI.

DROGO STARTED TO REACH OUT A HAND, THEN FLINCHED IN AGONY.
THE WOUNDS WERE WORSE THAN SER JORAH HAD LED HER TO BELIEVE.

WHERE ARE THE HEALERS?
THERE WERE TWO SORTS OF HEALERS IN THE KHALASAR: BARREN WOMEN AND EUNUCH SLAVES. THE FIRST FOR POTIONS AND SPELLS, THE OTHER FOR THE KNIFE, NEEDLE AND FIRE.

THE KHAL SENT THE HAIRLESS MEN AWAY.
MANY RIDERS ARE HURT.
LET THEM BE HEALED FIRST.

THE ARROW IS A FLY'S BITE. THIS LITTLE CUT, ONLY A NEW SCAR TO BOAST OF TO MY SON.

IT IS NOT FOR THE KHAL TO WAIT.
JHOGO! SEEK OUT THE EUNUCHS AND BRING THEM HERE AT ONCE.
SILVER LADY...

...I CAN HELP WITH THE GREAT RIDER'S HURTS.

THE KHAL NEEDS NO HELP FROM WOMEN WHO LIE WITH SHEEP! WE WILL CUT OUT HER TONGUE!

NO! SHE IS MINE. LET HER SPEAK.
I MEANT NO WRONG, FIERCE RIDERS.
I AM NAMED MIRRI MAZ DUUR, GODWIFE OF THIS TEMPLE.

MAEGI.
A MAEGI WAS A WOMAN WHO LAY WITH DEMONS. A VILE THING, EVIL AND SOULLESS.

THE WOMAN DIDN'T LOOK LIKE A MAEGI TO HER.
WHAT HEALING DO YOU KNOW?
MY MOTHER WAS GODWIFE BEFORE ME AND TAUGHT ME THE SONGS AND HOW TO MAKE SMOKES AND OINTMENTS.

WHEN I WAS YOUNGER, I WENT TO ASSHAI TO LEARN FROM THE MAGES. A MOONSINGER FROM JOGOS GAVE ME HER BIRTHING SONG, AND A MAESTER FROM THE SUNSET LANDS SHOWED ME ALL THE SECRETS THAT HIDE BENEATH THE SKIN.

A MAESTER?
MARWYN, HE NAMED HIMSELF. HE CAME FROM BEYOND THE SEA AND WORE A CHAIN OF MANY METALS.

SUCH MEN DO KNOW MUCH HEALING.
ALL MEN ARE ONE FLOCK, OR SO WE ARE TAUGHT.
I WILL HEAL YOUR GREAT RIDER.

WE ARE NO SHEEP, MAEGI!
THE ARROW MUST COME OUT, QOTHO.

AND YOUR BREAST MUST BE WASHED AND SEWN, LEST IT FESTER.
DO IT, THEN.

MY TOOLS AND POTIONS ARE INSIDE THE GOD'S HOUSE. WHERE THE HEALING POWERS ARE STRONGEST.

I WILL CARRY YOU, BLOOD OF MY BLOOD.
I NEED NO MAN'S HELP.

I AM NO MAN, MY SUN-AND-STARS. YOU MAY LEAN ON ME.

BEST IF YOU WAIT OUTSIDE.
WE WAIT HERE. KNOW THIS. HARM THE KHAL AND YOU SHALL SUFFER THE SAME.

IF YOU MUST STAY, THEN HELP. HOLD HIM DOWN WHILE I DRAW THE ARROW.

DROGO CURSED THE WOMAN AS SHE POURED THE HEATED WINE OVER HIS WOUNDS AND DREW THE ARROW FROM HIS ARM. SHE CLOSED HIS WOUNDS WITH A SILVER NEEDLE AND SILKEN THREAD.
WHEN SHE WAS DONE, SHE PAINTED THE SKIN WITH RED OINTMENT AND COVERED IT WITH LEAVES AND BOUND THE BREAST IN A RAGGED PIECE OF LAMBSKIN.

DRINK NEITHER WINE NOR MILK OF THE POPPY. YOU MUST KEEP YOUR BODY STRONG TO FIGHT THE POISON SPIRITS.
I AM KHAL. I SPIT ON PAIN AND DRINK WHAT I LIKE.

BEFORE, I HEARD YOU SPEAK OF BIRTHING SONGS.
I KNOW EVERY SECRET OF THE BLOODY BED, NOR HAVE I EVER LOST A BABE.

MY TIME IS NEAR. I WOULD HAVE YOU ATTEND ME, IF YOU WILL.
MOON OF MY LIFE, YOU DO NOT ASK A SLAVE. YOU *TELL* HER.
THIS PLACE IS ASHES. IT IS TIME TO RIDE.

REMEMBER, MAEGI! AS THE KHAL FARES, SO SHALL *YOU!*

AS YOU SAY, RIDER.
THE GREAT SHEPHERD GUARDS THE FLOCK.

ARE YOU WELL, SNOW?
WELL! WELL!

I... AM, MY LORD.
AND YOU?
IT WAS A LIE. THE PAIN OF HIS BURNS WAS STILL HIDEOUS, AND THE DREAMS WERE WORSE. BUT HE DARED NOT TELL MORMONT THAT.

DYWEN AND HAKE RETURNED LAST NIGHT. THEY FOUND NO SIGN OF YOUR UNCLE.
I KNOW.

IT WOULD SEEM THERE WERE ONLY TWO OF THOSE... CREATURES. THERE WILL BE MORE. I CAN FEEL IT, AND MAESTER AEMON AGREES.
SUMMER IS AT AN END, AND A WINTER IS COMING SUCH AS THIS WORLD HAS NEVER SEEN.
WINTER IS COMING. THE STARK WORDS.

THERE WAS A BIRD LAST NIGHT. WAS IT... WORD OF MY FATHER?
FATHER! FATHER!

IF THERE WAS NEWS OF LORD EDDARD, DON'T YOU THINK I WOULD HAVE SENT FOR YOU?
BASTARD OR NO, YOU ARE STILL HIS BLOOD.
THE MESSAGE CONCERNED SER BARRISTAN SELMY.
IT SEEMS HE'S BEEN REMOVED FROM THE KINGSGUARD.
THE FOOLS SENT SOME WATCHMEN TO SEIZE HIM, BUT HE SLEW TWO OF THEM AND ESCAPED.

WE HAVE WHITE SHADOWS IN THE WOODS AND UNQUIET DEAD STALKING OUR HALLS, AND A **BOY** SITS THE IRON THRONE.
BOY! BOY!

AND WHAT OF MY SISTERS?
PERHAPS THEY NEVER GOT MY LETTER. I FEAR WE COUNT FOR LESS THAN NOTHING IN KING'S LANDING.
THEY TELL US WHAT THEY WANT US TO KNOW, AND THAT IS LITTLE ENOUGH.

*AND YOU TELL ME WHAT YOU WANT **ME** TO KNOW, AND THAT'S LESS.*

HIS BROTHER ROBB HAD RIDDEN SOUTH TO WAR, YET NO WORD HAD BEEN BREATHED TO HIM...SAVE BY SAM, WHO'D READ THAT LETTER TO MAESTER AEMON.
SAM THEN WHISPERED ITS CONTENTS TO JON IN SECRET, ALL THE TIME SAYING HE SHOULDN'T.
HOW SOON DOES MAESTER AEMON SAY YOU'LL HAVE USE OF THAT HAND AGAIN?
CORN! CORN! CORN!
SOON.
GOOD. YOU'LL BE READY FOR THIS, THEN.

THE FIRE MELTED THE SILVER OFF THE POMMEL AND BURNT THE CROSSGUARD, BUT YOU'D NEED A FIRE A HUNDRED TIMES AS HOT TO HARM THE BLADE.

I HAD THE REST MADE ANEW.

THE MORMONTS HAVE CARRIED IT FOR FIVE CENTURIES. I PASSED IT TO MY SON WHEN I TOOK THE BLACK.
YOUR SON—
HE IS GIVING ME HIS SON'S SWORD...
HE HAD THE GRACE TO LEAVE IT BEHIND WHEN HE FLED, AND MY SISTER RETURNED IT TO MY KEEPING.
THE ORIGINAL POMMEL WAS A BEAR'S HEAD, SILVER. BUT FOR YOU, I THOUGHT A WHITE WOLF MORE APT.
ONE OF OUR BUILDERS IS A FAIR STONECARVER.
MY LORD, YOU HONOR ME. BUT—
SPARE ME YOUR BUT'S, BOY. YOU FOUGHT BRAVELY...AND MORE TO THE POINT, YOU THOUGHT QUICKLY.
"FIRE! WE OUGHT TO HAVE KNOWN. WE OUGHT TO HAVE REMEMBERED.
"EIGHT THOUSAND YEARS IS A GOOD WHILE, TO BE SURE...YET IF THE NIGHT'S WATCH DOES NOT REMEMBER, WHO WILL?"
WHO WILL! WHO WILL!

A SWORD IS SMALL PAYMENT FOR A LIFE. SO TAKE IT, AND THANK ME NO THANKS. HONOR THE STEEL WITH DEEDS, NOT WORDS.
DOES IT HAVE A NAME, MY LORD?
IT DID, ONCE. LONGCLAW, IT WAS CALLED.
CLAW! CLAW!
LONGCLAW IS AN APT NAME. WOLVES HAVE CLAWS, AS MUCH AS BEARS.
YOU'LL WANT TO WEAR THAT OVER THE SHOULDER. IT'S TOO LONG FOR THE HIP—AT LEAST UNTIL YOU'VE PUT ON A FEW INCHES.
ONCE YOUR HAND'S HEALED, YOU'LL NEED TO WORK AT DOUBLE-HAND STRIKES WITH SER ENDREW.
SER ENDREW?
SER ENDREW TARTH IS ON HIS WAY FROM THE SHADOW TOWER TO BECOME OUR NEW MASTER-AT-ARMS. SER ALLISER THRONE IS BRINGING THE HAND YOUR GHOST TOOK TO KING'S LANDING.
THAT SHOULD GET THIS BOY KING'S ATTENTION.

AND IT PUTS A THOUSAND LEAGUES BETWIXT HIM AND YOU WITHOUT SEEMING A REBUKE—THOUGH DON'T THINK THAT MEANS I APPROVE OF THAT NONSENSE IN THE COMMON HALL.
YES, SIR.

THAT'S A MAN'S SWORD, AND IT WILL TAKE A MAN TO WIELD HER.
I'LL EXPECT YOU TO ACT THE PART, HENCEFORTH.
YES, MY LORD.

NOW BACK TO YOUR DUTIES. THE NIGHT WILL BE COLD. I'LL WANT HOT SPICED WINE.
AND TELL HOBB IF HE SENDS ME BOILED MUTTON AGAIN, I'LL BOIL HIM.

YOU EARNED THAT, SNOW.
JON KNEW HE SHOULD BE PLEASED, YET HE DID NOT FEEL IT. THE TASTE OF ANGER WAS IN HIS MOUTH, THOUGH HE COULD NOT SAY WHO HE WAS ANGRY WITH OR WHY.

WELL, COME ABOUT. LET'S HAVE A LOOK.
AT WHAT?
YOUR ROSY BUTT CHEEKS. THE **SWORD**.

YOU KNEW?
I HELPED PATE CARVE THE STONE FOR THE POMMEL. SAM BOUGHT THE GARNETS IN MOLE'S TOWN.

WE KNEW BEFORE THAT. RUDGE WAS IN THE FORGE WHEN THE OLD BEAR BROUGHT IN THE BURNED BLADE.
THE ***SWORD!***

SWORD! SWORD! SWORD!

JON TRIED TO SEEM AS PROUD AND PLEASED AS HE OUGHT TO HAVE FELT, BUT NONE OF THE OTHERS HAD EYES FOR ANYTHING BUT THE BLADE.

IT'S VALYRIAN STEEL.
I HEARD OF A MAN WHO HAD A RAZOR OF VALYRIAN STEEL. CUT HIS OWN HEAD OFF TRYING TO SHAVE.
THE NIGHT WATCH IS THOUSANDS OF YEARS OLD, BUT I'LL WAGER LORD SNOW'S THE FIRST EVER HONORED FOR BURNING DOWN THE LORD COMMANDER'S TOWER.

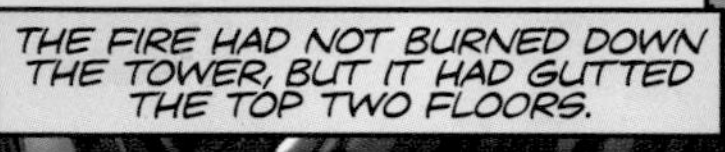
THE FIRE HAD NOT BURNED DOWN THE TOWER, BUT IT HAD GUTTED THE TOP TWO FLOORS.

THE OTHER WIGHT HAD BEEN CUT TO PIECES BY A DOZEN SWORDS. BUT NOT BEFORE IT HAD KILLED JAREMY RYKKER AND FOUR OTHERS.
STRENGTH AND COURAGE DID NOT AVAIL MUCH AGAINST FOEMEN WHO WERE ALREADY DEAD.

I NEED TO SEE HOBB ABOUT THE OLD BEAR'S SUPPER.
HIS FRIENDS MEANT WELL, BUT THEY DID NOT UNDERSTAND.

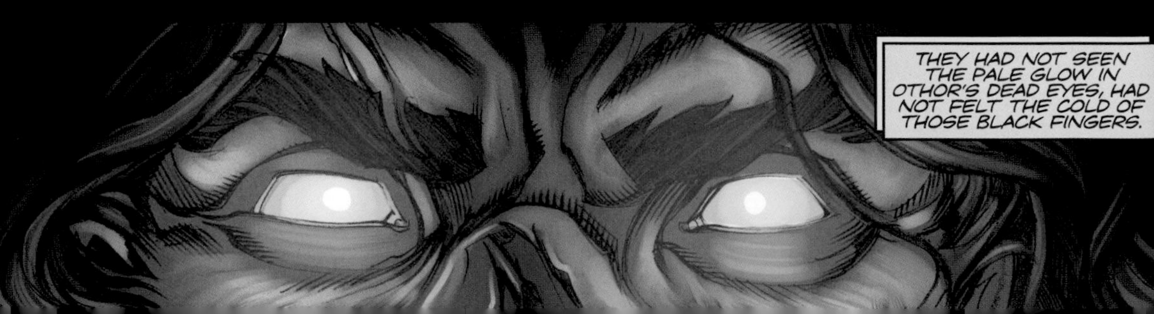
THEY HAD NOT SEEN THE PALE GLOW IN OTHOR'S DEAD EYES, HAD NOT FELT THE COLD OF THOSE BLACK FINGERS.

THEY WEREN'T WAITING ON WORD OF THEIR IMPRISONED FATHER, OR THEIR ENDANGERED SISTERS. THEIR BROTHERS WEREN'T LEADING ARMIES TO THE FIGHTING IN THE RIVERLANDS.
HOW COULD THEY HOPE TO COMPREHEND?

AND HOW COULD HE TELL LORD MORMONT THAT IT WAS ANOTHER MAN'S SWORD HE DREAMT OF?
LORD EDDARD STARK IS MY FATHER...

LOOK, IT'S YOU.
YOU'RE THE ONE THAT DESERVES THE HONOR.

JON REMEMBERED THE DAY SO LONG AGO WHEN THEY'D FOUND THE WOLVES. HEARING A NOISE, AND TURNING BACK TO SEE THE WHITE PUP ALONE.
HE'D BEEN DIFFERENT FROM HIS LITTER MATES, SO THEY DROVE HIM OUT.
JON?

SAM. HAVE YOU COME TO SEE THE SWORD TOO?
I...
AH...

MAESTER AEMON WANTS TO SEE YOU.
WHY?
YOU TOLD HIM, DIDN'T YOU? YOU TOLD HIM THAT YOU TOLD ME.
I...HE... JON, I THINK HE KNEW. HE SEES THINGS NO ONE ELSE SEES.
HE'S BLIND!
I CAN FIND THE WAY MYSELF.

SAM SAID YOU WANTED ME?
I DID INDEED. HERE. TAKE THIS BUCKET.

TOSS MEAT INTO THE CAGES. THE BIRDS WILL DO THE REST.

LORD MORMONT'S RAVEN LIKES FRUIT AND CORN.
HE IS A RARE BIRD. MOST PREFER FLESH. IT MAKES THEM STRONG, THOUGH I FEAR THEY RELISH THE TASTE OF BLOOD.

DOVES AND PIGEONS CAN ALSO CARRY MESSAGES, BUT THE RAVEN IS STRONGER, BOLDER, MORE CLEVER. SOME ABHOR THEM BECAUSE THEY ARE BLACK AND EAT THE DEAD.
THE NIGHT'S WATCH PREFERS RAVENS.

DID YOU EVER WONDER WHY THE MEN OF THE NIGHT WATCH TAKE NO WIVES AND FATHER NO CHILDREN?
NO.

SO THEY WILL NOT LOVE.

IF THE DAY COMES WHEN LORD EDDARD MUST CHOOSE BETWEEN HONOR AND THOSE HE LOVES, WHAT WOULD HE DO?
HE WOULD DO WHAT IS RIGHT.
THEN HE IS A MAN IN TEN THOUSAND.
WHAT IS DUTY AGAINST A NEWBORN SON? A BROTHER'S SMILE? A WOMAN'S LOVE? WIND AND WORDS.
"THE MEN WHO FORMED THE NIGHT WATCH KNEW THAT ONLY THEIR COURAGE SHIELDED THE REALM. THEY KEPT THEIR PLEDGE TO TAKE NO PART IN THE BATTLES OF THOSE THEY GUARDED."
"HOW EASY IT SEEMS TO WALK THE PATH OF HONOR. YET THE DAY COMES IN EVERY MAN'S LIFE WHEN IT IS NOT EASY. THE DAY COMES WHEN HE MUST CHOOSE."
AND THIS IS MY DAY. IS THAT WHAT YOU'RE SAYING?
IT HURTS, BOY. CHOOSING ALWAYS HURTS. I KNOW.
YOU DON'T KNOW. EVEN IF I AM A BASTARD, HE'S STILL MY FATHER!

DO YOU THINK YOU ARE THE FIRST? THREE TIMES, THE GODS SAW FIT TO TEST MY VOWS, AND THE LAST WAS AS CRUEL AS THE FIRST.
MY RAVENS WOULD BRING THE NEWS FROM THE SOUTH. THE RUIN OF MY HOUSE. THE DEATH OF MY KIN.
THEY CUT DOWN MY BROTHER'S POOR GRANDSON, AND **HIS** SON, AND EVEN THE LITTLE CHILDREN...
WHO ARE YOU?
A MAESTER OF THE CITADEL, BOUND TO THE NIGHT'S WATCH.
BUT MY FATHER WAS MAEKAR, FIRST OF HIS NAME. MY BROTHER AEGON REIGNED AFTER HIM IN MY STEAD.
AEMON... ***TARGARYEN?***
ONCE. SO YOU SEE, I **DO** KNOW...AND KNOWING, I WILL NOT TELL YOU STAY OR GO. YOU MUST MAKE THAT CHOICE YOURSELF AND LIVE WITH IT THE REST OF YOUR DAYS.
AS I HAVE...

ISSUE #21

PERHAPS I'D BEST CHARGE YOU WITH BURYING OUR DEAD, TYRION. IF YOU ARE AS LATE TO BATTLE AS TO TABLE, THE FIGHTING WILL BE DONE BEFORE YOU ARRIVE.
THE STARK HOST HAS MOVED SOUTH FROM THE TWINS. LORD FREY'S LEVIES HAVE JOINED THEM. THEY ARE LIKELY NO MORE THAN A DAY'S MARCH NORTH OF US.
PLEASE, FATHER. I'M ABOUT TO EAT.
DOES THE THOUGHT OF FACING THE STARK BOY UNMAN YOU? HE IS A GREEN BOY, MORE LIKE TO BE BRAVE THAN WISE.
IF YOUR SAVAGES SHARE YOUR RELUCTANCE, WE'LL HAVE WASTED GOOD STEEL ON THEM.
I SAW THE GREAT HAIRY ONE TODAY WHO INSISTED HE MUST HAVE **TWO** BATTLE AXES.
SHAGGA LIKES TO KILL WITH EITHER HAND. MY SAVAGES WILL PUT YOUR STEEL TO EXCELLENT USE.
WE HAD A THOUGHT TO PUT YOU AND YOUR WILDLINGS IN THE VANGUARD.
THE VANGUARD?

TYRION HAD A GLOOMY FEELING HE KNEW WHICH.
THEY SEEM FEROCIOUS ENOUGH.
LET ME TELL YOU HOW FEROCIOUS THEY ARE. LAST NIGHT A MOON BROTHER STABBED A STONE CROW OVER A SAUSAGE. TODAY, THREE STONE CROWS OPENED HIS THROAT FOR HIM.
BRONN BARELY MANAGED TO KEEP SHAGGA FROM CHOPPING OFF HIS COCK.
IF MY SON'S MEN HAVE NO DISCIPLINE, PERHAPS THE VANGUARD IS NOT THE PLACE FOR THEM.
DO ME NO KINDNESSES, FATHER.

IF YOU HAVE NO OTHER COMMAND TO OFFER ME, I'LL LEAD YOUR VAN.
I SAID NOTHING ABOUT COMMAND.

YOU WILL SERVE UNDER SER GREGOR.

I FIND I AM NOT HUNGRY AFTER ALL. PRAY EXCUSE ME.

OF HIS FORCE. EVERY CLAN HAD ITS OWN COOK FIRE. STONE CROWS DID NOT EAT WITH MOON BROTHERS, BLACK EARS DID NOT EAT WITH STONE CROWS, NO ONE ATE WITH BURNED MEN.

AT THE END OF THE DAY'S RIDE, HE'D SENT BRONN TO FIND HIM A LIKELY WHORE. ONE WHO KNEW WHO HE WAS. AND WHAT HE WAS.
WHERE DID YOU FIND HER?

I TOOK HER FROM A KNIGHT. THE MAN WAS LOATH TO GIVE HER UP, BUT YOUR NAME CHANGED HIS THINKING.
THAT AND MY DIRK AT HIS NECK.
I SEEM TO RECALL SAYING "FIND ME A WHORE," NOT "MAKE ME AN ENEMY."
THE PRETTY ONES WERE ALL CLAIMED. I CAN TAKE HER BACK IF YOU'D PREFER A TOOTHLESS DRAB.
DID YOU PERCHANCE NOTE THE NAME OF THE MAN YOU TOOK HER FROM? I'D RATHER NOT HAVE HIM BESIDE ME IN BATTLE.

YOU'LL HAVE ME BESIDE YOU, DWARF.
THEN SEE THAT I SURVIVE THE BATTLE, AND YOU CAN NAME YOUR REWARD.
MY FATHER'S PUT ME IN THE VANGUARD.
I'D DO THE SAME. A SMALL MAN WITH A LARGE SHIELD? YOU'LL GIVE THE ARCHERS FITS.

I FIND YOU ODDLY CHEERING, BRONN.
I AM TYRION, OF HOUSE LANNISTER. MEN CALL ME THE IMP.

MY MOTHER NAMED ME SHAE. MEN CALL ME... OFTEN.

SHALL I TAKE MY GOWN OFF?
IN GOOD TIME. GOLD I HAVE IN PLENTY, AND YOU'LL FIND ME GENEROUS.

BUT I'LL WANT MORE THAN WHAT'S BETWEEN YOUR LEGS, THOUGH I'LL WANT THAT TOO.
YOU'LL SHARE MY TENT, POUR MY WINE, LAUGH AT MY JESTS, RUB THE ACHE FROM MY LEGS. AND WHETHER I KEEP YOU A DAY OR A YEAR, YOU WILL TAKE NO OTHER MEN INTO YOUR BED.

FAIR ENOUGH.
WHEN HE ENTERED HER SHE WELCOMED HIM WITH WHISPERED ENDEARMENTS. HE SUSPECTED HER DELIGHT WAS FEIGNED BUT SHE DID IT SO WELL THAT IT DID NOT MATTER.
THAT MUCH TRUTH HE DID NOT CRAVE.
HE HAD NEEDED HER. HER OR SOMEONE LIKE HER. IT HAD BEEN NIGH ON A YEAR SINCE HE'D LAIN WITH A WOMAN.
HE COULD WELL DIE ON THE MORROW OR THE DAY AFTER.
HE FELT THE SOFTNESS OF HER BODY AGAINST HIS. A SONG FILLED HIS HEAD.
QUIETLY, HE BEGAN TO WHISTLE.
WHAT'S THAT M'LORD?

NOTHING. A SONG I LEARNED AS A BOY.
THEN MAN WHO BRONN TOOK YOU FROM. WHO WAS HE?

THE MINOR RETAINER OF AN INSIGNIFICANT LORDLING. YOU NEED NOT FEAR HIM, M'LORD. HE IS A SMALL MAN.

AND WHAT AM I, PRAY? A GIANT?

OH YES. MY GIANT OF LANNISTER.
AND FOR A TIME SHE ALMOST MADE HIM BELIEVE IT...

BAROOOOO
WAKE UP, M'LORD!
I'M FRIGHTENED.
THOSE ARE MY FATHER'S HORNS.
FIND MY ARMOR! QUICKLY!
THE STARK BOY STOLE A MARCH ON US. THEY'RE FORMING UP LESS THAN A MILE NORTH OF HERE.
SEE THAT THE CLANSMEN ARE READY TO RIDE.
IF I DIE, WEEP FOR ME.
MY LORD LOOKS FEARSOME.
M'LORD LOOKS LIKE A DWARF IN MISMATCHED ARMOR.
BUT I THANK YOU FOR YOUR KINDNESS.

THAT RIVER IS OURS! LET NO ENEMY COME BETWEEN US AND OUR RIVER!
HALFMAN!
HALFMAN!
HALFMAN!
CROW FOOD.

HE HAD NO TIME TO THINK ABOUT IT. SUDDENLY THE ENEMY WAS THERE.
GODS BE DAMNED, TYRION THOUGHT. LOOK AT THEM ALL.

HIS BATTLE SHRUNK TO THE FEW FEET OF GROUND AROUND HIS HORSE.
A MAN-AT-ARMS THRUST AT HIS CHEST, BUT TYRION RODE THE MAN DOWN.

TYRION RAINED AXE BLOWS DOWN ON THE ENEMY SHIELDS AND BODIES.
FOR A TIME, HE LOST HIMSELF.

WHEN HE FOUND A MOMENT'S RESPITE, HE REINED UP AND LOOKED FOR THE RIVER. IT WAS OFF TO HIS RIGHT. SOMEHOW, HED GOTTEN TURNED AROUND.

THE NORTHMEN'S FORMATION WAS CRUMBLING, FOOTMEN REELING BACK UNDER THE IMPACT OF THE MOUNTED ASSAULT.
HE HAD ONLY A GLIMPSE OF THE FIELD, AND THEN THE ENEMY WAS UPON HIM.

DWARF! DIE!

YOU DIE!
WINTERFELL!

FOR EDDARD AND WINTERFELL!

CRASH
TYRION THE IMP! DO YOU YIELD?
YIELD OR DIE!
NEEEEEEE
SMALL USE YOU TURNED OUT TO BE.
YOU DID WELL ENOUGH ON YOUR OWN.
YOU'VE LOST THE SPIKE FROM YOUR HELM.

NOT LOST. I KNOW WHERE IT IS.
HAVE YOU SEEN MY HORSE?

A FINE VICTORY! YOUR WILD MEN FOUGHT WELL.
DID THAT UPSET THE PLAN? WE WERE SUPPOSED TO BE BUTCHERED, WERE WE NOT?

I PUT THE LESS DISCIPLINED ON THE LEFT, YES. I'D HOPED THAT IF STARK SAW OUR LEFT COLLAPSE, HE MIGHT PLUNGE INTO THE GAP AND BE TAKEN.
A PITY MY SAVAGES RUINED YOUR DANCE.

A VICTORY IS A VICTORY.
MY LIEGE!
WE HAVE TAKEN SOME OF THEIR COMMANDERS. LORD CERWYN, HARRION KARSTARK. BUT ROOSE BOLTON HAS ESCAPED.
AND THE BOY?
THE YOUNG STARK WAS NOT WITH THEM. HE HAS THE GREATER PART OF THE HORSE, RIDING HARD FOR RIVERRUN.

THE WOODS WERE FULL OF WHISPERS.
MOONLIGHT WINKED ON THE TUMBLING WATERS OF THE STREAM BELOW. WARHORSES PAWED THE MOIST, LEAFY GROUND. MEN MADE NERVOUS JESTS IN HUSHED VOICES.
NOW AND AGAIN, SHE HEARD THE CHINK OF SPEARS. THE FAINT METALLIC SLITHER OF CHAIN MAIL. BUT EVEN THOSE SOUNDS WERE MUFFLED.
IT SHOULD NOT BE LONG NOW, MY LADY.
IT WILL COME WHEN IT COMES.
WHEN IT CAME, IT WOULD MEAN DEATH. HAL'S PERHAPS. OR HERS. OR ROBB'S.
NO ONE WAS SAFE. NO LIFE WAS CERTAIN.
THE KINGSLAYER HAD THEM THREE TO ONE, BUT HE LACKED PATIENCE.
AND CATELYN WAS NO STRANGER TO WAITING.

I MUST RIDE DOWN THE LINE, MOTHER. FATHER SAYS YOU SHOULD LET THE MEN SEE YOU BEFORE A BATTLE.
TO GIVE THEM COURAGE.
GO THEN. LET THEM SEE YOU.
AND WHO WILL GIVE ME COURAGE, SHE WONDERED.
WHEN ROBB HAD FORCED HER TO ACCEPT PROTECTORS, SHE HAD INSISTED THAT HE BE GUARDED AS WELL.
THE SONS OF HIS BANNERMEN HAD CLAMORED FOR THE HONOR.
WOULD SIX BE ENOUGH? WOULD SIX THOUSAND BE ENOUGH?
A BIRD CALLED IN THE DISTANCE. A SNOW SHRIKE. A NORTHERN BIRD.
THEY ARE COMING, MY LADY. GODS BE WITH US.
IF ROBB WAS FRIGHTENED, HE GAVE NO SIGN OF IT.
LET HIM KNOW SIXTEEN, AND TWENTY, AND FIFTY, SHE THOUGHT. LET HIM HOLD HIS OWN SON IN HIS ARMS.
PLEASE, PLEASE, PLEASE.

THE WOODS AROUND THEM GREW STILL. IN THE QUIET, SHE COULD HEAR THEM.
THE TREAD OF MANY HORSES. THE RATTLE OF SWORDS, SPEARS AND ARMOR. A LAUGH. A CURSE.
SHE SAW HIM ONLY FOR AN INSTANT, AND YET SHE KNEW HIM. JAIME LANNISTER WAS UNMISTAKABLE.
MAEGE MORMONT'S WAR HORN TOLD THAT THE LAST OF LANNISTER'S RIDERS HAD ENTERED THE TRAP. GREY WIND HOWLED IN ANSWER.
AAAAAOOOOOOOO
FOR A MOMENT, SHE FELT SOMETHING LIKE PITY FOR THE LANNISTERS BELOW.
THE WHISPERING WOOD LET OUT ITS BREATH ALL AT ONCE, AND THE NIGHT ERUPTED IN THE SCREAMS OF MEN AND HORSES.
WINTERFELL!
CATELYN WAITED, AS SHE HAD WAITED BEFORE. FOR BRANDON AND NED AND HER FATHER. THE REST HAD MELTED AWAY INTO THE TREES.

THE VALLEY RANG WITH ECHOES. THE CRACK OF A BROKEN LANCE, THE CLASH OF SWORDS.
HOOFBEATS. IRON BOOTS SPLASHING IN SHALLOW WATER.
MEN SHOUTING CURSES AND BEGGING FOR MERCY. THE TERRIFIED SCREAMING OF A THOUSAND HORSES.
GREY WIND'S HOWLS.
THE RIDGES PLAYED STRANGE TRICKS WITH SOUND.
ONCE SHE HEARD ROBB'S VOICE AS CLEAR AS IF HE WERE AT HER SIDE, CALLING TO ME! TO ME!

LITTLE BY LITTLE, THE SOUNDS DWINDLED AND DIED UNTIL THERE WAS ONLY THE WOLF.
AS THE RED DAWN BROKE IN THE EAST, GREY WIND BEGAN TO HOWL AGAIN.

ROBB! YOU'RE HURT!
NO. THIS IS TORRHEN'S BLOOD... OR...
I DON'T KNOW.
LADY STARK. I WOULD OFFER YOU MY SWORD BUT I SEEM TO HAVE MISLAID IT.
IT IS NOT YOUR SWORD I WANT. GIVE ME MY FATHER. MY BROTHER. MY HUSBAND AND DAUGHTERS.

I HAVE MISLAID THEM AS WELL, I FEAR.

A PITY.

KILL HIM, ROBB. TAKE HIS HEAD OFF.
HE'S MORE USE ALIVE. AND MY LORD FATHER NEVER CONDONED THE MURDER OF PRISONERS.

PUT HIM IN IRONS. AND PUT A STRONG GUARD ON HIM. LORD KARSTARK WILL WANT HIS HEAD ON A PIKE.
THAT HE WILL.
WHY SHOULD LORD KARSTARK WANT HIM DEAD?
LORD KARSTARK'S SONS. HE KILLED THEM BOTH.

NO ONE CAN FAULT LANNISTER ON HIS COURAGE. WHEN HE SAW ALL WAS LOST, HE RALLIED HIS RETAINERS AND AND FOUGHT HIS WAY TOWARD LORD ROBB.
HE ALMOST MANAGED.

HE MISLAID HIS SWORD IN EDDARD KARSTARK'S NECK AFTER HE TOOK OFF TORRHEN'S HAND AND SPLIT DARRYN HORNWOOD'S SKULL OPEN.
IF THEY HADN'T TRIED TO STOP HIM—

THEN I SHOULD BE MOURNING INSTEAD OF LORD KARSTARK.
YOUR MEN DID WHAT THEY WERE SWORN TO DO, ROBB.

GRIEVE FOR THEM. HONOR THEIR VALOR. BUT NOT NOW.
YOU HAVE NO TIME FOR GRIEF. YOU HAVE CUT THE HEAD OFF THE SNAKE, BUT THREE QUARTERS OF THE BODY IS STILL COILED AROUND MY FATHER'S CASTLE.
WE HAVE WON A BATTLE, NOT A WAR.
BUT SUCH A BATTLE. MY LADY, THE REALM HAS NOT SEEN SUCH A VICTORY SINCE THE FIELD OF FIRE. I VOW THE LANNISTERS LOST TEN MEN FOR EVERY ONE OF OURS THAT FELL.

AND LORD TYWIN? IS HE FALLEN?
UNTIL HE IS, THIS WAR IS FAR FROM DONE.

MY MOTHER IS RIGHT. WE STILL HAVE RIVERRUN.

THE SCENT OF HOT BREAD DRIVING ALONG THE STREET OF FLOUR WAS SWEETER THAN ANY PERFUME ARYA HAD SMELLED.
IT WAS ALSO THE BEST PLACE TO CATCH PIGEONS. THEY CAME FOR THE CRUMBS. AND COMPARED TO CATCHING CATS, PIGEONS WERE EASY.
THREE COPPERS.
I'LL TRADE YOU A FAT PIGEON.
THE OTHERS TAKE YOUR PIGEON. YOU KEEP YOUR HANDS TO YOURSELF.
THE GOLD CLOAKS KNOW HOW TO DEAL WITH THIEVING GUTTER RATS.
IN FLEA BOTTOM, THERE WERE POT-SHOPS WHERE HUGE TUBS OF STEW HAD BEEN SIMMERING FOR YEARS AND YOU COULD TRADE YOUR BIRD FOR A "BOWL O' BROWN."
ARYA WOULD HAVE GIVEN ANYTHING FOR A CUP OF MILK AND A LEMON CAKE, BUT THE BROWN WASN'T SO BAD–AS LONG AS YOU DIDN'T THINK ABOUT THE MEAT.

EVERY DAY SINCE HER ESCAPE, ARYA HAD VISITED THE SEVEN CITY GATES IN TURN. BUT THE GUARDS LET NO ONE OUT.
SOMETIMES SHE THOUGHT ABOUT SWIMMING THE RIVER OR STOWING AWAY ON A SHIP.
WHEN SHE SAW GUARDSMEN IN THE GREY AND WHITE OF WINTERFELL, IT BROUGHT TEARS TO HER EYES. SHE COULDN'T READ THE NAME WRITTEN ON THE HULL, BUT SHE HAD TO KNOW.

PLEASE? WHAT SHIP IS THIS?
SHE'S THE **WIND WITCH** OUT OF MYR.

SHE'S STILL **HERE?**
THE SHIP HER FATHER HAD HIRED TO TAKE HER HOME, STILL WAITING. SHE'D IMAGINED IT SAILED LONG AGO.

LOOK WITH YOUR EYES, SYRIO WHISPERED IN HER MEMORY.

SHE KNEW HER FATHER'S MEN. THE THREE IN GREY WERE STRANGERS.
YOU! WHAT DO YOU WANT, BOY?

IT WAS A TRAP, AND IT WAS ALL SHE COULD DO NOT TO BOLT AWAY.
WANT TO BUY A PIGEON?

GET OUT OF HERE.
SHE DID AS HE TOLD HER. SHE DIDN'T HAVE TO PRETEND TO BE FRIGHTENED

FLEA BOTTOM HAD A STENCH TO IT. A STINK OF PIGSTIES AND STABLES AND TANNER'S SHEDS. ARYA WOUND HER WAY THROUGH THE MAZE OF STREETS DULLY.
SHE'D LOST THE PIGEON ALONG THE WAY.
SHE'D HAVE TO WALK ALL THE WAY BACK TO THE STREET OF FLOUR TO GET ANOTHER ONE AS FAT.
BONG
BONG
BONG
BONG
BONG
BONG
THE BELLS AGAIN? IS IT THE BOY KING THAT'S DIED NOW?
THAT'S A BOY FOR YOU. THEY NEVER LAST LONG.
STUPID SLUT. KING'S NOT DEAD. THAT'S ONLY **SUMMONING** BELLS.

WAIT! WHAT'S HAPPENING?
THEY'RE CARRYING THE HAND TO THE SEPT! BUU SAYS THEY'RE TAKING HIS HEAD OFF!

BONG
...CARRYING LORD STARK UP TO BAELOR'S SEPT.
BONG
BONG
PAST TIME, THE TRAITOR.
EVERYONE WAS MOVING IN THE SAME DIRECTION, ALL IN A HURRY TO SEE WHAT THE RINGING WAS ABOUT. ARYA JOINED THE STREAM OF PEOPLE.
BY THE TIME THEY REACHED THE STREET OF THE SISTERS, THEY WERE PACKED SHOULDER TO SHOULDER.
SINCE WHEN DO THEY KNICK TRAITORS ON THE STEPS OF THE SEPT?
WELL THEY DON'T MEAN TO ANOINT HIM KNIGHT. I HEARD IT WAS STARK KILLED KING ROBERT.
AT THE TOP OF VISENYA'S HILL, THE WHITE MARBLE PLAZA WAS A SOLID MASS OF PEOPLE, ALL YAMMERING AT EACH OTHER AND STRAINING TO GET CLOSER.
SHE FOUND HERSELF PRESSED INTO A PLINTH WITH BAELOR THE BLESSED, THE SEPTON KING, LOOKING DOWN AT HER, AND SHE CLIMBED UP TO WEDGE HERSELF BETWEEN HIS FEET.
THAT WAS WHEN SHE SAW HER FATHER.

THE BELL CEASED ITS TOLL.
A QUIET SETTLED ACROSS THE GREAT PLAZA.
I AM EDDARD STARK, LORD OF WINTERFELL AND HAND OF THE KING.
I COME BEFORE YOU TO CONFESS MY TREASON IN THE SIGHT OF GODS AND MEN.
...NO...
I BETRAYED THE TRUST OF MY KING AND FRIEND. I PLOTTED TO DEPOSE HIS SON AND TAKE THE THRONE FOR MYSELF. LET THE HIGH SEPTON AND THE SEVEN BEAR WITNESS.
JOFFREY BARATHEON IS THE ONE TRUE HEIR, AND BY GRACE OF THE GODS, LORD OF THE SEVEN KINGDOMS.
THE CROWD BEGAN TO SCREAM. TAUNTS AND OBSCENITIES FILLED THE AIR.
AS WE SIN, SO DO WE SUFFER. THIS MAN HAS CONFESSED HIS SINS IN THE SIGHT OF GODS AND MEN IN THIS HOLY PLACE!
THE GODS ARE JUST, BUT THEY ARE ALSO MERCIFUL. WHAT SHALL BE DONE WITH THE TRAITOR, YOUR GRACE?

MY MOTHER BIDS ME LET LORD EDDARD TAKE THE BLACK. AND LADY SANSA HAS BEGGED MERCY FOR HER FATHER.
BUT THEY HAVE THE SOFT HEARTS OF WOMEN.

SO LONG AS I AM KING, TREASON SHALL NOT GO UNPUNISHED. SER ILYN! BRING ME HIS HEAD.
NO!

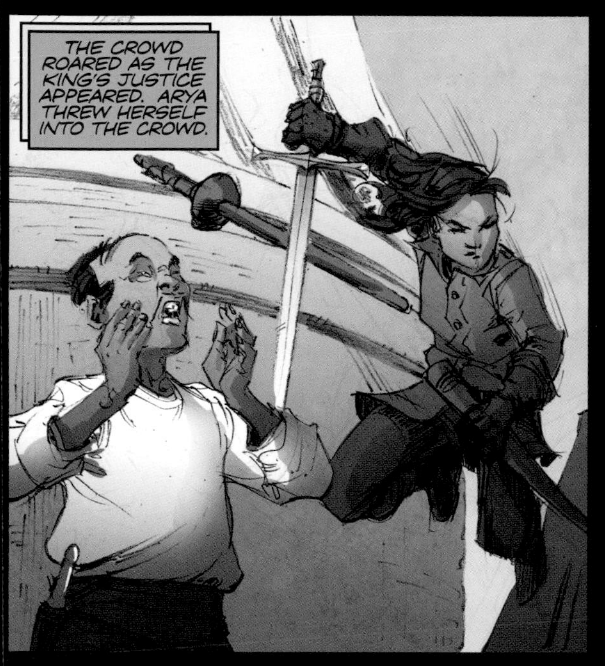
THE CROWD ROARED AS THE KING'S JUSTICE APPEARED. ARYA THREW HERSELF INTO THE CROWD.

BODIES CLOSED IN AROUND HER, PUSHING AND TRAMPLING.

SHE BOWLED PAST, SHOVING PEOPLE ASIDE. SQUIRMING BETWEEN THEM, SLAMMING INTO ANYONE IN HER WAY.

IT WAS NO GOOD. NO GOOD. THERE WERE TOO MANY PEOPLE. NO SOONER DID A HOLE OPEN THAN IT CLOSED AGAIN.

DON'T LOOK!
"SHUT YOUR MOUTH AND CLOSE YOUR EYES, BOY."

YES. YOU REMEMBER ME, DON'T YOU, BOY?
AND SHE DID. YOREN, HIS NAME WAS. THE BLACK BROTHER WHO'D COME TO VISIT HER FATHER.

"YOU'LL BE COMING WITH ME, BOY. AND YOU'LL BE KEEPING YOUR MOUTH SHUT."

I'M NOT–
NOT A SMART BOY?

"THAT WHAT YOU MEAN TO SAY?"

"DON'T LOOK!"

ISSUE #22

SANSA GAVE HERSELF OVER TO DARKNESS. SHE SLEPT, WOKE WEEPING, THEN SLEPT AGAIN.
WHEN SHE COULD NOT SLEEP, SHE LAY UNDER HER BLANKETS AND SHIVERED WITH GRIEF.
THE SERVING GIRLS TRIED TO TALK TO HER WHEN THEY BROUGHT HER MEALS. GRAND MAESTER PYCELLE HAD COME ONCE WITH HIS FLASKS AND BOXES.
HE LEFT HER A FLASK OF HONEYWATER AND HERBS AND TOLD HER TO DRINK A SWALLOW EVERY NIGHT. SHE DRANK IT ALL RIGHT THEN AND WENT BACK TO SLEEP.
PERHAPS I WILL DIE TOO, SHE TOLD HERSELF. THE THOUGHT DID NOT SEEM TOO TERRIBLE.
SHE IMAGINED HER BODY ON THE STONES BELOW, BROKEN AND INNOCENT, SHAMING THOSE WHO BETRAYED HER.

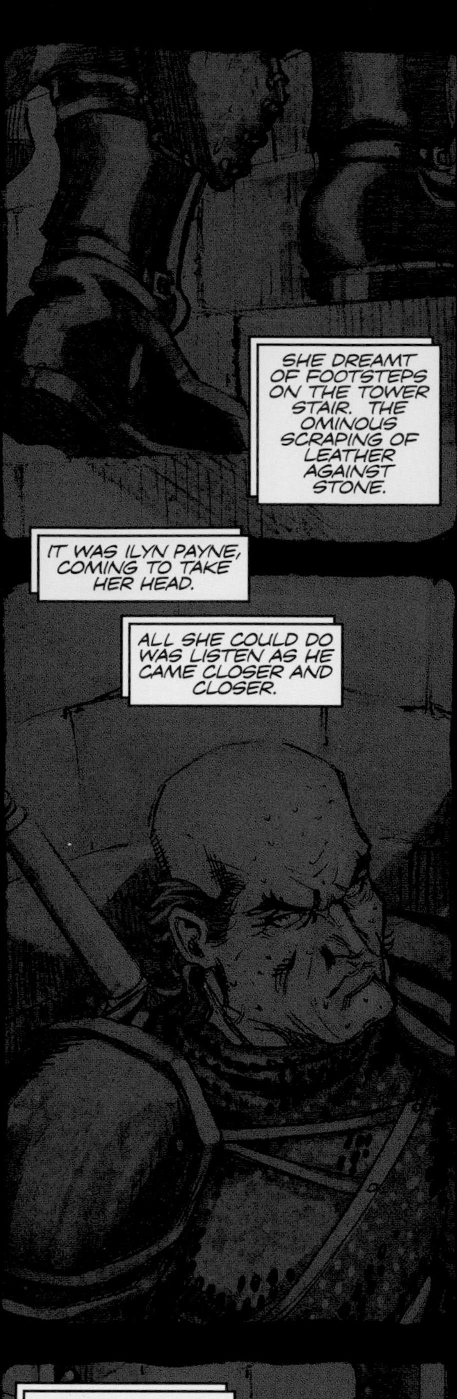
SHE DREAMT OF FOOTSTEPS ON THE TOWER STAIR. THE OMINOUS SCRAPING OF LEATHER AGAINST STONE.
IT WAS ILYN PAYNE, COMING TO TAKE HER HEAD.
ALL SHE COULD DO WAS LISTEN AS HE CAME CLOSER AND CLOSER.

THERE WAS NO PLACE TO RUN. NO WAY TO BAR THE DOOR. NO ONE TO HEAR HER PLEAS.

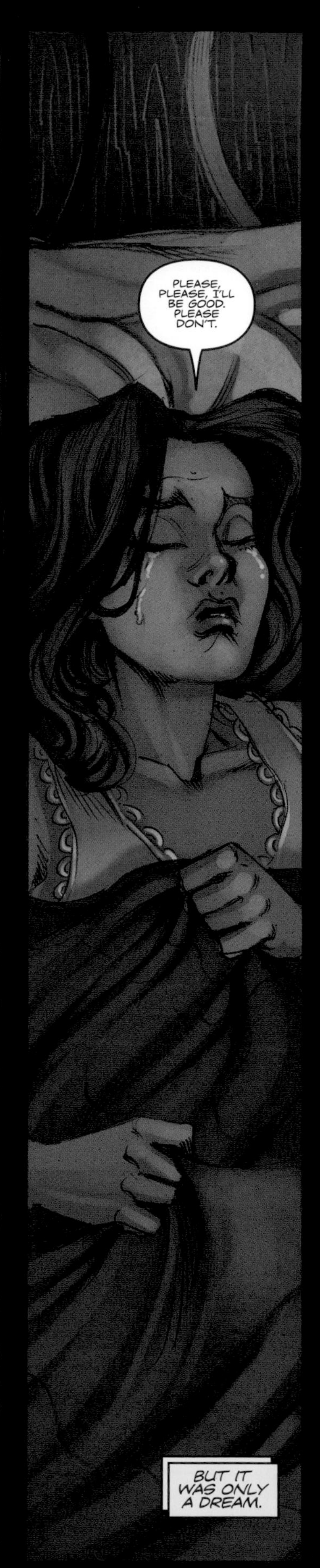
PLEASE, PLEASE, I'LL BE GOOD. PLEASE DON'T.
BUT IT WAS ONLY A DREAM.

WHEN THEY CAME FOR HER IN TRUTH, SANSA NEVER HEARD THEIR FOOTSTEPS.
GET UP. YOU WILL ATTEND ME IN COURT THIS AFTERNOON.
SEE THAT YOU BATHE AND DRESS AS BEFITS MY BETROTHED.
NO. PLEASE. LEAVE ME BE.
IF YOU WON'T RISE AND DRESS YOURSELF, MY HOUND WILL DO IT FOR YOU.
I BEG OF YOU, MY PRINCE...

I'M KING NOW.
DOG, GET HER OUT OF BED.
AH!

DO AS YOU'RE BID, CHILD.
DRESS.

I DID AS THE QUEEN ASKED. I WROTE WHAT SHE TOLD ME.
PLEASE LET ME GO HOME. I WON'T DO ANY TREASON. I ONLY WANT TO GO HOME!

...AS IT PLEASE YOU.

IT DOES **NOT** PLEASE ME. MOTHER SAYS I'M STILL TO MARRY YOU, SO YOU'LL STAY HERE AND OBEY.
I DON'T **WANT** TO MARRY YOU! YOU CHOPPED OFF MY FATHER'S HEAD!

YOU PROMISED YOU'D BE **MERCIFUL!**

HE WAS A TRAITOR!
I NEVER PROMISED TO SPARE HIM, AND I WAS MERCIFUL.

IF HE HADN'T BEEN YOUR FATHER, I'D HAVE HAD HIM TORN OR FLAYED, BUT I GAVE HIM A CLEAN DEATH INSTEAD.
IT WAS AS IF SHE WERE SEEING HIM FOR THE FIRST TIME. SHE WONDERED HOW SHE COULD EVER HAVE THOUGHT HIM HANDSOME.

HIS LIPS WERE AS SOFT AND RED AS THE WORMS YOU FOUND AFTER A RAIN, AND HIS EYES WERE VAIN AND CRUEL.
I HATE YOU.

MY MOTHER TELLS ME IT ISN'T FITTING THAT A KING STRIKE HIS WIFE.
SER MERYN?

PAK

WILL YOU OBEY NOW, OR SHALL I HAVE HIM CHASTISE YOU AGAIN?

I... AS...AS YOU COMMAND, MY LORD.
YOU MUST CALL ME **YOUR GRACE** NOW.

SAVE YOURSELF SOME PAIN, GIRL. GIVE HIM WHAT HE WANTS.

WHAT... DOES HE WANT? PLEASE TELL ME.
HE WANTS YOU TO SMILE AND SMELL SWEET AND BE HIS LADY LOVE THE WAY THE SEPTA TAUGHT YOU.
HE WANTS YOU TO LOVE HIM...

...AND FEAR HIM.

AFTER HE WAS GONE, SANSA WAITED, STARING AT THE WALL, UNTIL HER BED MAIDS CAME.

I WILL NEED HOT WATER FOR MY BATH, PLEASE.
AND POWDER TO HIDE THIS BRUISE.

THE HOT WATER MADE HER THINK OF WINTERFELL. SHE TOOK STRENGTH FROM THAT.
SHE HAD NOT WASHED SINCE THE DAY HER FATHER DIED. SHE WAS STARTLED AT HOW FILTHY THE WATER BECAME.

HER MAIDS SLUICED THE BLOOD OFF HER FACE, WASHED HER HAIR, AND BRUSHED IT.
SHE DID NOT SPEAK TO THEM EXCEPT TO GIVE COMMANDS. THEY WERE LANNISTER SERVANTS.

MY LADY. HIS GRACE HAS INSTRUCTED ME TO ESCORT YOU TO THE THRONE ROOM.
DID HE INSTRUCT YOU TO HIT ME IF I REFUSED TO COME?

ARE YOU REFUSING, MY LADY?
HE DID NOT HATE HER. NEITHER DID HE LOVE HER. SHE WAS ONLY A **THING** TO HIM.

I SHALL DO WHATEVER HIS GRACE COMMANDS.
AS I DO.
YES, BUT YOU ARE NO TRUE KNIGHT.
SANDOR CLEGANE WOULD HAVE LAUGHED AT THAT, SHE KNEW.
OTHER MEN MIGHT HAVE CURSED HER, WARNED HER TO KEEP SILENT, BEGGED HER FORGIVENESS.
SER MERYN TRANT SIMPLY DID NOT CARE.
THE BALCONY WAS DESERTED SAVE FOR HER. SHE STOOD FIGHTING TO HOLD BACK TEARS.
BELOW JOFFREY SAT ON HIS IRON THRONE AND DISPENSED WHAT IT PLEASED HIM TO CALL JUSTICE

NINE CASES OUT OF TEN SEEMED TO BORE HIM. THOSE HE ALLOWED HIS COUNCIL TO HANDLE. BUT WHEN HE DID CHOOSE TO RULE, NOT EVEN HIS QUEEN MOTHER COULD SWAY HIM.
A THIEF WAS BROUGHT BEFORE HIM, AND HE HAD SER ILYN CHOP HIS HAND OFF RIGHT THERE IN COURT.
TWO KNIGHTS CAME WITH A DISPUTE OVER LAND, AND HE DECREED THAT THEY SHOULD DUEL ON THE MORROW. TO THE DEATH.
THE LAST CASE WAS A PLUMP TAVERN SINGER ACCUSED TO MAKING A SONG THAT RIDICULED THE LATE KING ROBERT. JOFFREY GAVE HIM A DAY TO CHOOSE WHETHER TO KEEP HIS FINGERS OR HIS TONGUE.

BUT HER ORDEAL WAS NOT YET DONE.
YOU LOOK MUCH BETTER THAN YOU DID. WALK WITH ME.

THE TOUCH OF HIS HAND WOULD HAVE THRILLED HER ONCE. NOW IT MADE HER FLESH CRAWL.
MY NAME DAY WILL BE HERE SOON. THERE WILL BE A GREAT FEAST. AND GIFTS.

WHAT ARE YOU GOING TO GIVE ME?

I... I HAD NOT THOUGHT, MY LORD.
YOUR GRACE. YOU REALLY ARE A STUPID GIRL, AREN'T YOU? MY MOTHER SAYS SO.

SHE DOES?
SHE WORRIES ABOUT OUR CHILDREN. WHETHER THEY'LL BE STUPID LIKE YOU. I TOLD HER NOT TO TROUBLE HERSELF.

I'LL GET YOU WITH CHILD, AND IF THE FIRST ONE'S STUPID, I'LL CHOP OFF YOUR HEAD AND FIND A SMARTER WIFE.
THIS WAY.

SUDDENLY SHE KNEW WHERE THEY WERE GOING.
NO! PLEASE, DON'T MAKE ME. I BEG YOU!
I CAN HAVE SER MERYN DRAG YOU UP. YOU WON'T LIKE THAT.
SHE COULD ALMOST HEAR THE REST OF IT. HE'LL HAVE YOU UP THERE NO MATTER WHAT, SO GIVE HIM WHAT HE WANTS.
DO IT, GIRL.
THE CLIMB WAS SOMETHING FROM A NIGHTMARE. EVERY STEP WAS A STRUGGLE, AND THERE WERE MORE STEPS THAN SHE WOULD HAVE BELIEVED. A THOUSAND THOUSAND STEPS.
AND HORROR WAITING ON THE RAMPARTS...

FROM THE HIGH BATTLEMENTS OF THE GATEHOUSE, THE WHOLE WORLD SPREAD OUT BEFORE HER. BEYOND THE WALLS WAS OPEN COUNTRY, FIELDS AND FORESTS.
AND BEYOND THAT, NORTH AND NORTH AND NORTH AGAIN, STOOD WINTERFELL...

WHAT ARE YOU LOOKING AT? THIS IS WHAT I WANTED YOU TO SEE, RIGHT HERE.

THIS ONE IS YOUR FATHER.
DOG, TURN IT AROUND SO SHE CAN SEE HIM.

HE CAN MAKE ME LOOK, SANSA THOUGHT, BUT HE CANNOT MAKE ME SEE.
THE HEAD HAD BEEN DIPPED IN TAR TO PRESERVE IT LONGER. IT DID NOT REALLY LOOK LIKE LORD EDDARD.
IT DID NOT EVEN LOOK REAL.

HOW LONG DO I HAVE TO LOOK?
DO YOU WANT TO SEE THE REST?
IF IT PLEASE YOUR GRACE.
I'M KEEPING THOSE TWO FOR STANNIS AN MY UNCLE RENLY.
THAT'S YOUR SEPTA, THERE.
WHY DID YOU KILL HER? SHE WAS GODSWORN—
SHE WAS A TRAITOR.
AND YOU HAVEN'T SAID WHAT YOU MEAN TO GIVE ME FOR MY NAME DAY.
MAYBE I SHOULD GIVE SOMETHING TO YOU. WOULD YOU LIKE THAT?
IF IT PLEASE YOU, MY LORD.
YOUR BROTHER IS A TRAITOR, TOO. THAT'S WHAT I'LL GIVE YOU. YOUR BROTHER'S HEAD.
OR MAYBE MY BROTHER WILL GIVE ME YOURS!

A TRUE WIFE DOES NOT MOCK HER LORD.
SER MERYN, TEACH HER.
THIS TIME, HE HELD HER HEAD STILL AS HE STRUCK HER.
HE HIT HER TWICE. HER LIP SPLIT, BLOOD MIXING WITH THE SALT OF TEARS.
YOU SHOULDN'T BE CRYING ALL THE TIME. WIPE OFF THE BLOOD. YOU'RE ALL MESSY.

THE OUTER PARAPET CAME TO HER CHIN. ALONG THE INNER WALKWAY, THERE WAS NOTHING BUT A LONG PLUNGE TO THE BAILEY, EIGHTY FEET BELOW.
YOU COULD DO IT, SHE TOLD HERSELF. ALL IT WOULD TAKE WAS A SHOVE.
IT WOULDN'T EVEN MATTER IF SHE WENT OVER WITH HIM.

HERE, GIRL.
AND THEN THE MOMENT WAS GONE.

THANK YOU.
SHE WAS A GOOD GIRL, AND SHE ALWAYS REMEMBERED HER COURTESIES.

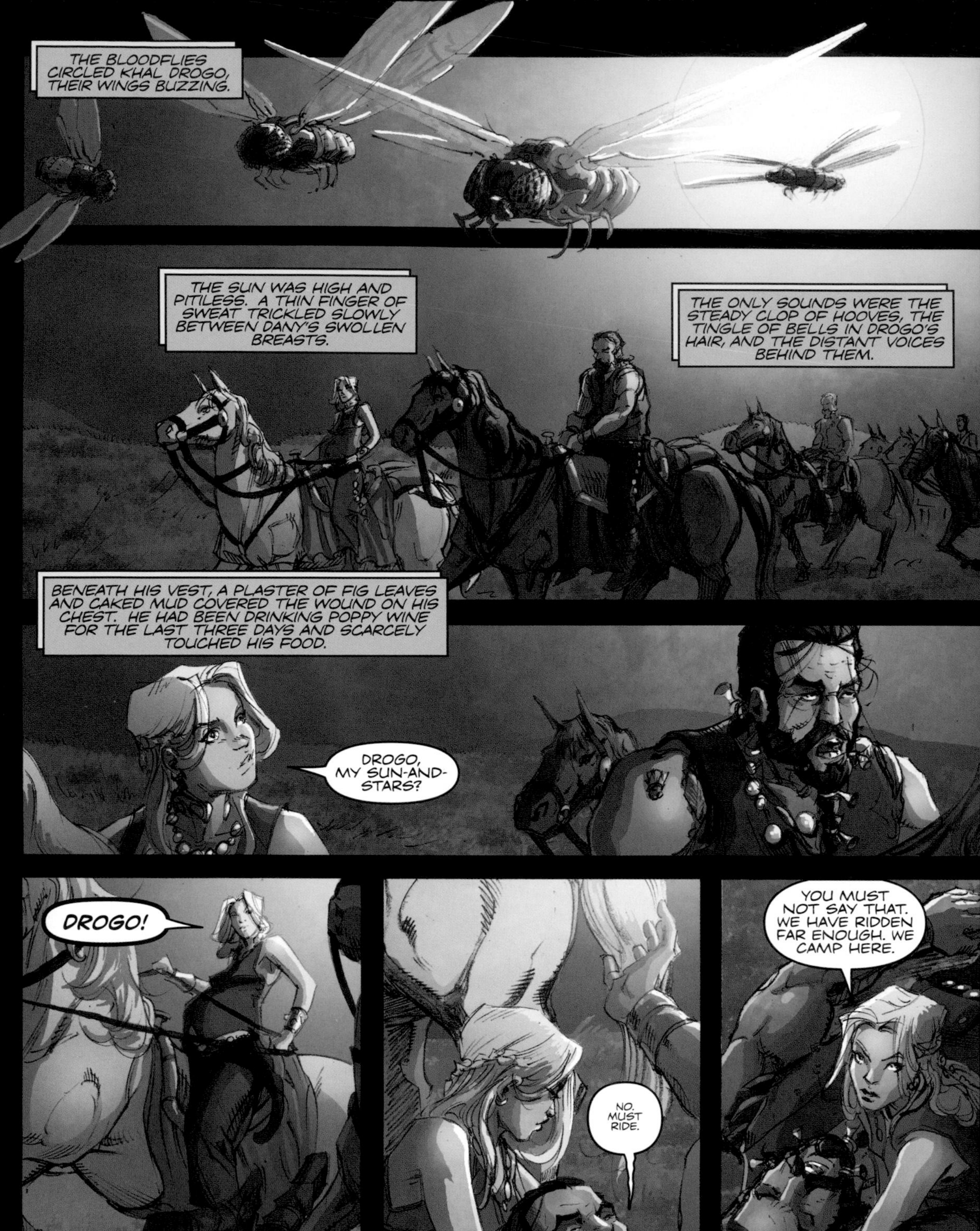
THE BLOODFLIES CIRCLED KHAL DROGO, THEIR WINGS BUZZING.
THE SUN WAS HIGH AND PITILESS. A THIN FINGER OF SWEAT TRICKLED SLOWLY BETWEEN DANY'S SWOLLEN BREASTS.
THE ONLY SOUNDS WERE THE STEADY CLOP OF HOOVES, THE TINGLE OF BELLS IN DROGO'S HAIR, AND THE DISTANT VOICES BEHIND THEM.
BENEATH HIS VEST, A PLASTER OF FIG LEAVES AND CAKED MUD COVERED THE WOUND ON HIS CHEST. HE HAD BEEN DRINKING POPPY WINE FOR THE LAST THREE DAYS AND SCARCELY TOUCHED HIS FOOD.
DROGO, MY SUN-AND-STARS?

DROGO!
NO. MUST RIDE.
HE FELL FROM HIS HORSE.
YOU MUST NOT SAY THAT. WE HAVE RIDDEN FAR ENOUGH. WE CAMP HERE.

THIS IS NO CAMPING GROUND.
IT IS NOT FOR A WOMAN TO BID US HALT. NOT EVEN A KHALEESI.

WE CAMP **HERE**, HAGGO. TELL THEM KHAL DROGO COMMANDED THE HALT BECAUSE MY TIME IS NEAR AND I COULD NOT CONTINUE.
COHOLLO, BRING THE SLAVES TO PUT UP THE KHAL'S TENT.

QOTHO, BRING ME MIRRI MAZ DUUR.
THE ***MAEGI?*** THIS I WILL NOT DO.

YOU WILL, OR WHEN DROGO WAKES, HE WILL HEAR WHY YOU DEFIED ME!

SHE KNEW HE WOULD RETURN WITH THE HEALER, HOWEVER LITTLE HE MIGHT LIKE IT.
THE SLAVES PLACED THE TENT AND LAID PATTERNED CARPETS ON THE GROUND. IT WAS STIFLING UNDER THE SANDSILK.

HE DIES.
THE KHAL CANNOT DIE. HE IS FATHER OF THE STALLION WHO MOUNTS THE WORLD. HE STILL WEARS THE BELLS HIS FATHER GAVE HIM.
HE **FELL** FROM HIS HORSE.

SHE HAD A BATH BROUGHT TO COOL HIS BURNING SKIN. WHILE THEY SWEETENED THE SULFER-STINKING WATER WITH BITTER OILS AND MINT LEAVES, SHE TENDED KHAL DROGO.
HE FELL FROM HIS HORSE. SHE HAD SEEN IT.

DANY KNEW WHAT IT MEANT. A KHAL WHO COULD NOT RIDE COULD NOT RULE.

KHALEESI. THE ANDAL IS COME.
HELP HIM. FOR THE LOVE YOU BEAR ME, HELP HIM NOW.
SEND YOUR MAIDS AWAY.
WHEN THEY WERE ALONE, SER JORAH PRIED BACK THE PLASTER. A FOUL, SWEET SMELL ROSE FROM THE WOUND.
YOUR KHAL IS GOOD AS DEAD, PRINCESS.
HE CAN'T DIE. HE MUSTN'T. IT WAS ONLY A CUT—
SAVE YOUR TEARS, CHILD. WE DO NOT HAVE TIME FOR GRIEF. WE MUST GO, AND QUICKLY. BEFORE HE DIES.
WHEN DROGO IS GONE, THIS KHALASAR WILL TURN ON ITSELF, AND THE WINNER WILL WANT NO RIVALS.
YOUR BOY WILL BE FED TO THE DOGS AND YOU WILL BE TAKEN TO LIVE WITH THE CRONES AT VAES DOTHRAK.
I WILL NOT LEAVE HIM.
IT WAS TRUE. DROGO HAD BEEN MORE THAN HER SUN-AND-STARS. HE HAD BEEN THE SHIELD THAT KEPT HER SAFE.

THE WOUND HAS FESTERED.
THIS IS YOUR WORK, MAEGI!
TAKE HER OUTSIDE AND STAKE HER TO THE EARTH, TO BE THE MOUNT OF EVERY PASSING MAN.
STOP IT! I WILL NOT HAVE HER HARMED.
THE PRINCESS IS STILL YOUR KHALEESI, BLOODRIDER.
ONLY WHILE THE BLOOD-OF-MY-BLOOD STILL LIVES. WHEN HE DIES, SHE IS NOTHING.
WE WILL GO. FOR NOW.

SER JORAH, I MAY HAVE NEED OF YOUR SWORD. BEST GO DON YOUR ARMOR.
SO YOU HAVE SAVED ME ONCE MORE.
AND NOW YOU MUST SAVE HIM. PLEASE.
YOU DO NOT ASK A SLAVE. YOU TELL HER.
YET ASK OR TELL, IT MAKES NO MATTER. HE IS BEYOND THE HEALER'S SKILL.
ALL I CAN DO NOW IS EASE THE DARK ROAD BEFORE HIM.
NO. SAVE HIM. I WILL FREE YOU, I SWEAR IT.
YOU MUST KNOW A WAY. SOME MAGIC, SOME...
THERE IS A SPELL. BUT SOME WOULD SAY DEATH IS CLEANER.

"I LEARNED THE WAY IN ASSHAI, AND PAID DEAR FOR THE LESSON. MY TEACHER WAS A BLOODMAGE FROM THE SHADOW LANDS."

THEN YOU TRULY ARE A MAEGI?
ONLY A MAEGI CAN SAVE YOUR RIDER NOW, SILVER LADY.
BUT THERE IS A PRICE.
YOU'LL HAVE IT. GOLD. HORSES. WHATEVER YOU LIKE.

IT IS NOT A MATTER OF GOLD OR HORSES. THIS IS BLOODMAGIC. ONLY DEATH MAY PAY FOR LIFE.
DEATH? MY DEATH?
NOT YOUR DEATH, KHALEESI.
THEN DO IT.
AS YOU SPEAK, SO IT SHALL BE DONE. CALL YOUR SERVANTS. AND BRING HIS HORSE.

NO! MUST RIDE...
KHALEESI, THIS IS FORBIDDDEN. LET ME KILL THE MAEGI.

IN VAES DOTHRAK, KHAL DROGO SLEW A STALLION AND I ATE ITS HEART TO GIVE OUR SON STRENGTH.
THIS IS THE SAME. THE SAME!

STRENGTH OF THE MOUNT, GO INTO THE RIDER. STRENGTH OF THE BEAST, GO INTO THE MAN.
ONLY A HORSE, SHE TOLD HERSELF.

IF SHE COULD BUY DROGO'S LIFE WITH THE DEATH OF A HORSE, SHE WOULD PAY A THOUSAND TIMES OVER.

GO WITH THEM, SILVER LADY. MY SONG WILL WAKE POWERS OLD AND DARK. ONCE I BEGIN TO SING, NO ONE MUST ENTER THE TENT.
NO ONE WILL ENTER.

BRING HIM BACK TO ME.

WHAT HAVE YOU **DONE?** WE COULD HAVE FLED TO ASSHAI.
AM I TRULY YOUR PRINCESS?
YOU ARE, GODS SAVE US BOTH.
THEN HELP ME NOW.
A AI ILA LAII
MIRRI MAZ DUUR'S VOICE ROSE TO A HIGH, ULULATING WAIL THAT SENT A SHIVER DOWN DANY'S BACK.
THE DOTHRAKI BEGAN TO MUTTER AND BACK AWAY.
LAI AI ALA LAII
THROUGH THE BLOOD-SPATTERED SAND-SILK, DANY GLIMPSED SHADOWS MOVING.
MIRRI MAZ DUUR WAS DANCING, AND NOT ALONE.
THIS MUST NOT BE!

THIS WILL BE!

YOU WILL DIE FOR THIS. BUT THE OTHER MUST DIE FIRST.
NO! YOU MUSTN'T!

STOP HIM!
KILL HIM!

AI LA IAL IA

HORSE-LORD!

TRY ME.
COME THEN, CRAVEN! EUNUCH IN AN IRON SUIT!
YOU DIE NOW!
IN HER WOMB, HER SON KICKED WILDLY.
AI LAI LA LA!
THE DOTHRAKI WERE SHOUTING, MIRRI MAZ DUUR WAILING INSIDE THE TENT LIKE NOTHING HUMAN, QUARO PLEADING FOR WATER AS HE DIED.
DANY FELT A SHARP PAIN IN HER BELLY.

THERE WAS A WETNESS ON HER THIGHS.
SHE CRIED OUT FOR HELP, BUT NO ONE HEARD.
STOP. PLEASE, STOP, SHE WEPT. THE PRICE IS TOO HIGH.
NO! MY BABY!

TUK
EVEN AS COHOLLO DIED, AGONY SEIZED HER AND SQUEEZED LIKE A GIANT'S FIST.
HER BREATH WENT OUT OF HER. IT WAS ALL SHE COULD DO TO GASP.
THE CROWD WAS DISPERSING, THE DOTHRAKI STEALING SILENTLY BACK TO THEIR TENTS AND SLEEPING MATS. SOME WERE SADDLING HORSES AND RIDING OFF.
IT FELT AS IF HER SON HAD A KNIFE IN EACH HAND, AS IF HE WERE HACKING AT HER TO CUT HIS WAY OUT.
DOREAH! IRRI! CURSE YOU, COME **HERE!**
FETCH THE BIRTHING WOMEN!
THEY WILL NOT COME. THEY SAY SHE IS ACCURSED.
THEY'LL COME OR I'LL HAVE THEIR **HEADS!**

THEY ARE GONE, MY LORD.
THE LAMB WOMAN KNOWS THE SECRETS OF THE BIRTHING BED. SHE SAID SO.
NO, SHE TRIED TO SHOUT, BUT NO WHISPER ESCAPED HER LIPS. PLEASE, NO!
AI LA
DO NOT TAKE ME THERE! THE SHAPES! THE DANCERS!
SER JORAH CARRIED HER INTO THE TENT.
ALA IA

ISSUE #23

NO, NO, NO!
THEY DON'T FIGHT VERY WELL.
YOUR LORD FATHER TOOK THE CREAM OF HIS GUARD TO KING'S LANDING, AND YOUR BROTHER TOOK THE REST.
WE MUST HAVE MEN TO TAKE THEIR PLACES.
IF I STILL HAD MY LEGS, I COULD BEAT THEM ALL.
AND IF I HAD A POLEAXE, HODOR COULD BE MY LEGS.
I THINK THAT...UNLIKELY. WHEN A MAN FIGHTS, HIS ARMS AND LEGS AND THOUGHTS MUST BE AS ONE.
YOU MUST PUT THESE DREAMS ASIDE. THEY WILL ONLY BREAK YOUR HEART.
DREAMS.
I DREAMED ABOUT THE THREE-EYED CROW AGAIN LAST NIGHT. HE LED ME DOWN TO THE CRYPTS.
FATHER WAS THERE. HE WAS SAD.

AND WHY WAS THAT?
SOMETHING TO DO WITH JON, I THINK. BUT HODOR WON'T GO DOWN TO THE CRYPTS.
HODOR WON'T...
GO DOWN INTO THE CRYPTS. WHEN I WOKE, I TOLD HIM TO TAKE ME THERE, ONLY HE WOULDN'T GO DOWN.
WHY WOULD YOU GO DOWN TO THE CRYPTS?
TO SEE IF FATHER WAS THERE.

SWEET CHILD, ONE DAY LORD EDDARD WILL SIT BELOW, BUT NOW HE IS THE QUEEN'S PRISONER.
YOU WILL NOT FIND HIM IN THE CRYPTS.

HE WAS LAST NIGHT.
WOULD YOU LIKE TO GO AND SEE?

HODOR WON'T TAKE ME.
I BELIEVE I CAN SOLVE THAT.

THE WILDLING WOMAN OSHA WAS SUMMONED. BRAN DID NOT EVEN MIND THAT SHE CARRIED HIM IN HER ARMS AND NOT ON HER BACK.
HE COULD NOT REMEMBER THE LAST TIME HE HAD BEEN IN THE CRYPTS. WHEN HE WAS LITTLE, HE USED TO PLAY DOWN HERE WITH ROBB AND JON AND HIS SISTERS.

GRIM FOLKS, BY THE LOOK OF THEM.
THEY WERE THE KINGS OF WINTER.

WINTER'S GOT NO KING. IF YOU'D SEEN IT, YOU'D KNOW THAT, SUMMER BOY.

THEY WERE THE KINGS IN THE NORTH FOR THOUSANDS OF YEARS.
DO YOU RECALL YOUR HISTORY, BRAN? TELL OSHA WHO THEY WERE AND WHAT THEY DID, IF YOU CAN.

HE TOLD HER OF JON STARK, WHO DROVE THE SEA RAIDERS FROM THE EAST AND BUILT THE CASTLE AT WHITE HARBOR.
OF THEON STARK, CALLED THE HUNGRY WOLF BECAUSE HE WAS ALWAYS AT WAR. OF BRANDON THE SHIPWRIGHT, WHO SAILED ACROSS THE SUNSET SEA AND WAS NEVER SEEN AGAIN.
OF RODRIK STARK WHO WON BEAR ISLAND IN A WRESTLING MATCH. OF TORRHEN STARK, THE KING WHO KNELT, THE LAST KING IN THE NORTH AND THE FIRST LORD OF WINTERFELL.
AND OF HIS GRANDFATHER, LORD RICKARD, BEHEADED BY MAD KING AERYS.
THE MAID'S A FAIR ONE.
AUNT LYANNA. PRINCE RHAEGAR CARRIED HER OFF. ROBERT FOUGHT A WAR TO WIN HER BACK, BUT SHE DIED.
LORD EDDARD'S TOMB, FOR WHEN HIS TIME COMES. IS THIS WHERE YOU SAW YOUR FATHER IN YOUR DREAM?
YES.
AS YOU SEE, HE IS NOT HERE. DREAMS ARE ONLY DREAMS. THE TOMB IS EMP–
RRRRRRAAA

AAAH!
SUMMER!
RRRRRR
AAARRRR
YOU LET MY FATHER BE!
RICKON. MAESTER LUWIN DIDN'T DO ANYTHING TO FATHER.
FATHER'S NOT HERE.
YES HE IS. I SAW HIM LAST NIGHT.
THAT BEAST IS SUPPOSED TO BE CHAINED IN THE KENNELS!
I LET HIM LOOSE. SHAGGYDOG DOESN'T LIKE BEING CHAINED.

RICKON, WOULD YOU LIKE TO COME WITH ME? IT'S DARK HERE, AND COLD.
BUT I HAVE TO WAIT FOR FATHER.
WE'LL WAIT ELSEWHERE TOGETHER, YOU AND ME AND OUR WOLVES.

SHAGGYDOG IS TOO WILD TO RUN LOOSE. I'M THE THIRD MAN HE HAS SAVAGED. THE WOLF HAS TO BE CHAINED, OR...
OR KILLED, BRAN THOUGHT.
WE WILL WAIT IN YOUR TOWER.
THAT IS QUITE IMPOSSIBLE...
THE BOY'S THE LORDLING HERE, AS I RECALL. THE MAESTER'S TOWER IT IS.

THIS IS FOLLY. BRAN, YOU ARE OLD ENOUGH TO KNOW THAT DREAMS ARE ONLY DREAMS.
SOME ARE AND SOME AREN'T. THE CHILDREN OF THE FOREST COULD TELL YOU A THING OR TWO ABOUT DREAMING.
THE CHILDREN ARE DEAD AND GONE. THEY LIVE ONLY IN DREAMS, NOW.
AH! SEVEN HELLS, THAT HURTS.

IS THIS MADE OF GLASS?
DRAGON-GLASS.
OBSIDIAN. THE CHILDREN OF THE FOREST HUNTED WITH THAT, THOUSANDS OF YEARS AGO.
AND STILL DO.
THEY WERE THE PEOPLE OF THE DAWN AGE. BEFORE KINGS AND KINGDOMS.

"THEY LIVED IN THE DEPTH OF THE WOODS, IN CAVES AND SECRET TREE TOWNS. THEIR WISE MEN WERE CALLED GREENSEERS AND CARVED FACES IN THE WEIRWOODS TO KEEP WATCH."
"HOW LONG THE CHILDREN REIGNED HERE OR WHERE THEY CAME FROM, NO MAN CAN KNOW."
"BUT SOME TWELVE THOUSAND YEARS AGO, THE FIRST MEN APPEARED FROM THE EAST, CROSSING THE BROKEN ARM OF DORNE BEFORE IT WAS BROKEN.
"AS THE FIRST MEN CARVED OUT HOLDFASTS AND FARMS, THEY CUT DOWN THE FACES AND SET THEM TO FIRE."
"THE GREENSEERS USED DARK MAGICS TO RAISE THE SEAS AND SHATTER THE ARM, BUT TOO LATE. THE WARS WENT ON UNTIL THE EARTH RAN RED WITH BLOOD."
"FINALLY THE WISE OF BOTH RACES PREVAILED. THEY FORGED THE PACT THAT ENDED THE DAWN AGE AND BEGAN THE AGE OF HEROES."
"THE FIRST MEN WERE GIVEN THE COASTLAND, PLAINS, MEADOWS, MOUNTAINS AND BOGS. THE DEEP WOODS WERE TO REMAIN THE CHILDREN'S FOREVER."

SO THE CHILDREN OF THE FOREST ARE ALL GONE NOW?
HERE, THEY ARE. NORTH OF THE WALL, THINGS ARE DIFFERENT.
THE ANDALS CAME WITH THEIR SEVEN-POINTED STAR AND THEIR NEW GODS. THE SIX KINGDOMS FELL BEFORE THEM, AND THE CHILDREN FLED NORTH—
OOOOOOOO
SUMMER BEGAN TO HOWL.
OOOOOOOO
AAAAOOO
SHAGGYDOG ADDED HIS VOICE, AND DREAD CLUTCHED AT BRAN'S HEART.
IT'S COMING, HE THOUGHT. THE THREE-EYED CROW...
IT WAS ONLY A RAVEN, THOUGH. AND THE WOLVES CEASED HOWLING AS SUDDENLY AS THEY'D BEGUN.

IT'S INJURED. A HAWK, OR PERHAPS AN OWL.
A WONDER THE POOR THING GOT THROUGH.

WHAT... WHAT IS IT?

YOU KNOW WHAT IT IS, BOY.
WE... WE SHALL NEED TO FIND A STONECARVER WHO KNEW YOUR FATHER'S LIKENESS WELL.

THEY HAVE MY SON.
THEY DO, MY LORD.
HOW? EVEN AFTER THE WHISPERING WOOD, YOU HAD RIVERRUN SURROUNDED BY A GREAT HOST.
WHAT MADNESS MADE SER JAIME SPLIT HIS FORCES?
YOU HAVE NEVER SEEN RIVERRUN, OR YOU WOULD KNOW JAIME HAD LITTLE CHOICE.
I WOULD HAVE DONE THE SAME.

"TO CUT OFF ALL APPROACHES, YOU MUST HAVE A FORCE ON ALL THREE BANKS. THERE IS NO OTHER WAY."
WE'D BUILT PALISADES OF SHARPENED STAKES AROUND THE CAMPS, YET IT WAS NOT ENOUGH.
AND WE WERE TOLD THE STARK FORCE WAS EAST OF THE GREEN FORK–

YOUR OUTRIDERS SAW NOTHING? GAVE NO WARNING?
OUR OUTRIDERS HAD BEEN VANISHING, SER GREGOR. BUT THOSE WHO DID COME BACK HAD SEEN NOTHING.

A MAN WHO SEES NOTHING HAS NO USE FOR EYES. CUT THEM OUT AND GIVE THEM TO THE NEXT MAN.
TELL HIM YOU HOPE THAT FOUR EYES MIGHT SEE BETTER THAN TWO.

AND IF NOT, THE MAN AFTER HIM WILL HAVE SIX.

YOU SAID THEY CAME AT NIGHT?
YES, LORD KEVAN.

"BY THE TIME OUR MEN KNEW WHAT WAS HAPPENING, RIDERS WERE GALLOPING THROUGH THE CAMP, SWORDS AND TORCHES IN HAND."
"LORD BRAX LED US TO THE RAFTS AND TRIED TO POLE ACROSS, BUT THE CURRENT WAS AGAINST US, AND THE TULLYS STARTED FLINGING ROCKS FROM THEIR CATAPULTS."
"AND WHEN THEY SAW OUR MEN FORMING A SHIELD WALL, THEY LOWERED THEIR DRAWBRIDGE AND ATTACKED US FROM THE REAR."
"WHILE WE WERE TRYING TO CROSS, MORE STARKS SWEPT IN FROM THE WEST. THEY FREED OUR CAPTIVES, INCLUDING SER EDMURE TULLY, AND MADE OFF WITH THEM, THEN SET FIRE TO OUR SIEGE TOWERS."

THIS IS A CATASTROPHE! JAIME'S HOST IS ROUTED, AND THE STARKS AND TULLYS HAVE CUT US OFF FROM THE WEST.
IF THEY MARCH ON CASTERLY ROCK, WHAT'S TO STOP THEM?
MY LORDS, WE ARE BEATEN. WE MUST SUE FOR PEACE!
PEACE?
THERE'S YOUR PEACE, SER HARYS. MY SWEET NEPHEW BROKE IT FOR GOOD AND ALL WHEN HE ORNAMENTED THE RED KEEP WITH LORD EDDARD'S HEAD.
YOU'LL HAVE AN EASIER TIME DRINKING FROM THAT CUP THAN MAKING PEACE WITH ROBB STARK NOW.
HE'S WINNING, OR HADN'T YOU NOTICED?
TWO BATTLES DO NOT MAKE A WAR.
PERHAPS A TRUCE? TO ALLOW US TO TRADE OUR PRISONERS FOR THEIRS?
WHAT DO WE OFFER FOR MY BROTHER? EDDARD'S ROTTING HEAD?
I HEARD QUEEN CERSEI HAS THE HAND'S DAUGHTERS.
STARK WOULD BE AN ASS TO TRADE JAIME LANNISTER FOR TWO GIRLS!
WE MUST RANSOM SER JAIME, WHATEVER THE COST.
IF WE ASK FOR A TRUCE, THEY WILL THINK US WEAK.
SOMEONE MUST RETURN TO CASTERLY ROCK AND RAISE A FRESH HOST.

THEY HAVE MY SON!
TYRION, REMAIN. AND YOU AS WELL, SER KEVAN.
THE REST OF YOU... OUT.
YOU HAVE THE RIGHT OF IT, TYRION. ALIVE, WE MIGHT HAVE USED LORD EDDARD TO FORGE A PEACE AND DEAL WITH ROBERT'S BROTHERS. DEAD...
MADNESS. RANK MADNESS.
JOFF'S ONLY A BOY. AT HIS AGE, I COMMITTED A FEW FOLLIES OF MY OWN...
THEN I SUPPOSE WE SHOULD BE GRATEFUL HE HAS NOT YET MARRIED A WHORE.
OUR POSITION IS WORSE THAN YOU KNOW. IT WOULD SEEM WE HAVE A NEW KING.

A NEW... WHO? WHAT HAVE THEY DONE TO JOFFREY?
NOTHING... YET. BUT RENLY BARATHEON HAS WED MARGAERY TYRELL AT HIGHGARDEN AND CLAIMED THE CROWN.
MY DAUGHTER COMMANDS US TO RIDE FOR KING'S LANDING AT ONCE TO DEFEND AGAINST HIM.
COMMANDS.
HOW IS JOFFREY TAKING THE NEWS?
SHE HAS NOT SEEN FIT TO TELL HIM, FOR FEAR HE MIGHT LEAD THE CITY WATCH AGAINST RENLY HIMSELF.
IF HE TAKES THE WATCH, IT LEAVES THE CITY UNDEFENDED. AND WITH LORD STANNIS ON DRAGONSTONE...
YES. I HAD THOUGHT YOU WERE THE ONE MADE FOR MOTLEY, TYRION, BUT IT APPEARS I WAS WRONG.
WHY FATHER, THAT SOUNDS ALMOST LIKE PRAISE. AND WHAT OF STANNIS? HE'S THE ELDER, NOT RENLY.
WHIPERS AND RUMORS. STANNIS IS BUILDING SHIPS, STANNIS IS HIRING SELLSWORDS. YET HE DOES NOTHING.

ROBB STARK WILL HAVE THE LORDS OF THE TRIDENT WITH HIM, AND ROOSE BOLTON TO THE NORTH. IF WE REMAIN HERE, WE WILL BE CAUGHT BETWEEN THREE ARMIES.
YES, AND SO TOMORROW WE MUST MAKE FOR HARRENHAL.

WHY HARRENHAL? THAT IS A GRIM, UNLUCKY PLACE. SOME CALL IT CURSED.

LET THEM. UNLEASH SER GREGOR BEFORE US WITH HIS REAVERS. VARGO HOAT AND SER AMORY LORCH AS WELL.
I WANT TO SEE THE RIVERLANDS AFIRE FROM THE GODS EYE TO THE RED FORK.
THEN THEY WILL BURN, MY LORD. I SHALL GO AND GIVE THE COMMANDS.

YOUR SAVAGES MIGHT RELISH A BIT OF RAPINE. TELL THEM THEY MAY RIDE WITH VARGO HOAT.
I WOULD PREFER TO KEEP THEM WITH ME.

THEN YOU HAD BEST CONTROL THEM. I WILL NOT HAVE THE CITY PLUNDERED.
THE CITY? WHAT CITY WOULD THAT BE?

KING'S LANDING.
I AM SENDING YOU TO COURT.

AND WHAT AM I TO DO THERE?
RULE.
JOFFREY MUST BE TAKEN IN HAND BEFORE HE RUINS US, LURCHING FROM ONE FOLLY TO THE NEXT. MAKING JANOS SLYNT A LORD?
HIS FATHER WAS A BUTCHER, AND THEY GRANT HIM ***HARRENHAL***, THAT WAS THE SEAT OF KINGS!
AND DISMISSING SELMY? YES, HE WAS OLD, BUT HE LENT HONOR TO ANY MAN HE SERVED. UNLIKE THE HOUND...

IF CERSEI CANNOT CURB THE BOY, YOU MUST. AND IF HIS COUNCILORS ARE PLAYING FALSE—
SPIKES. HEADS. WALLS. I KNOW.
BUT WHY ME? WHY NOT A...***BIGGER*** MAN?

YOU ARE MY SON.

ONE LAST THING. YOU WILL NOT TAKE YOUR ***WHORE*** TO COURT.

M'LORD?
SHH. ALL'S WELL.
I HAVE A MIND TO TAKE YOU TO KING'S LANDING, SWEETLING.

WINGS SHADOWED HER FEVER DREAMS.
SHE KNEW WITH THE LOGIC OF DREAM THAT SHE COULD NOT—**MUST** NOT—LOOK BEHIND HER.
YOU DON'T WANT TO WAKE THE DRAGON, DO YOU?
GREAT WINGS CROSSED THE SKY, AND THE DOTHRAKI SEA TOOK FLAME.
...DON'T WANT TO WAKE THE DRAGON, DO YOU?
RHAEGAR WAS THE LAST DRAGON.
THE LAST DRAGON...
SHE FELT THE DARK BEHIND HER, AND THE RED DOOR SEEMED FARTHER AWAY THAN EVER.
THE DRAGON DOES NOT **BEG**, SLUT! YOU DO NOT **COMMAND** THE DRAGON!
FOR A MOMENT, HER SON STOOD BEFORE HER.
...WANT TO WAKE THE DRAGON, DO YOU...

SHE COULD FEEL THE COLD BEHIND HER, PROMISING DEATH THAT WAS MORE THAN DEATH.
SHE COULD FEEL THE HEAT INSIDE HER, A TERRIBLE BURNING IN HER WOMB.
AND IN AN INSTANT, HE WAS GONE, CONSUMED LIKE A MOTH BY A CANDLE.
HER TEARS TURNED TO STEAM WHERE THEY TOUCHED HER SKIN.
...WAKE THE DRAGON...
A KNIFE OF PAIN RIPPED DOWN HER BACK, AND SHE FLEW.
THE STONE WAS GONE AND SHE FLEW ACROSS THE DOTHRAKI SEA.
SHE COULD SMELL HOME. SHE COULD SEE IT, THERE, JUST BEYOND THE RED DOOR.
...THE DRAGON...
HER BROTHER RHAEGAR.
THE LAST DRAGON.
SHE WOKE TO THE TASTE OF ASHES.

JHIQUI. DOREAH.
MY THROAT IS DRY.

I HAVE BEEN SICK.
HOW LONG?

LONG.
THE WATER WAS WARM AND FLAT, BUT SHE DRANK IT EAGERLY.

BRING ME...I WANT TO HOLD...
OH, KHALEESI—

AN EGG. BRING ME A DRAGON'S EGG. I WANT TO HOLD IT.
AND MORE WATER.

SHE COULD FEEL A HEAT IN THE EGG. SURELY IT WAS ONLY THE FEVER STILL WITHIN HER, BUT IT SEEMED AS IF SOMETHING DEEP IN THE STONE TWISTED AND STRETCHED AT HER TOUCH.
IT DID NOT FRIGHTEN HER.

ALL HER FEAR HAD BEEN BURNED AWAY.
THE KHAL LIVES?

THE KHAL... LIVES.
TELL ME.
I SHALL BRING SER JORAH.

WHAT IS IT? DROGO... AND MY SON?
WHY HAD SHE NOT REMEMBERED THE CHILD UNTIL NOW?

THE BOY... DID NOT LIVE.
MY SON IS DEAD, SHE THOUGHT. BUT SHE HAD KNOWN IT, EVEN BEFORE SHE WOKE.

SHE SHOULD WEEP, BUT HER EYES WERE DRY AS ASH. ALL THE GRIEF HAD BEEN BURNED OUT OF HER.

SHE COULD FEEL RHAEGO RECEDING FROM HER AS IF HE HAD NEVER BEEN.
SER JORAH. COME HERE.
WHAT DO YOU FEEL? HEAT?
NO. SHELL HARD AS ROCK AND COLD AS STONE.
TELL ME HOW MY CHILD DIED.
HE NEVER LIVED.

MONSTROUS. TWISTED. I DREW HIM FORTH MYSELF.
HE WAS SCALED LIKE A LIZARD, BLIND, WITH THE STUB OF A TAIL AND SMALL LEATHER WINGS LIKE A BAT.

"AND HE WAS FILLED WITH GRAVEWORMS AND THE STINK OF CORRUPTION. DEATH WAS IN THAT TENT, KHALEESI."

I SAW ONLY YOU ALONE, MAEGI, DANCING WITH THE SHADOWS.
THE GRAVE CASTS LONG SHADOWS, AND NO LIGHT CAN HOLD THEM BACK.
YOU SAID ONLY DEATH WOULD PAY FOR LIFE. I THOUGHT YOU MEANT THE HORSE.
THAT WAS A LIE YOU TOLD YOURSELF. YOU KNEW THE PRICE.
AND THE PRICE WAS PAID. WHERE IS KHAL DROGO?
SHOW ME WHAT I BOUGHT WITH MY SON'S *LIFE*.
DROGO'S KHALASAR IS GONE.
THE DOTHRAKI ONLY FOLLOW THE STRONG. THERE WAS NO WAY TO HOLD THEM.
A KHAL WHO CANNOT RIDE IS NO KHAL.

WHY IS HE OUT HERE ALONE, IN THE SUN?
HE SEEMS TO LIKE THE WARMTH, PRINCESS. HIS EYES FOLLOW THE SUN.
HE CAN WALK AFTER A FASHION. HE WILL EAT IF YOU PUT FOOD IN HIS MOUTH, DRINK IF YOU DRIBBLE WATER ON HIS LIPS.
LEAVE US, ALL OF YOU. I WOULD SPEAK TO THE MAEGI ALONE.

YOUR SPELLS ARE COSTLY, MAEGI.
YOU ASKED FOR LIFE. YOU PAID FOR LIFE. HE LIVES.

THIS IS NOT LIFE FOR ONE SUCH AS DROGO! WHEN WILL HE BE AS HE WAS?

WHEN THE SUN RISES IN THE WEST AND SETS IN THE EAST.
WHEN THE SEAS GO DRY AND MOUNTAINS BLOW IN THE WIND LIKE LEAVES.
WHEN YOUR WOMB QUICKENS AGAIN AND YOU BEAR A LIVING CHILD.
THEN HE WILL RETURN, AND NOT BEFORE.
YOU KNEW WHAT I WAS BUYING. YOU KNEW THE PRICE, AND YET YOU LET ME PAY IT?
THE STALLION WHO MOUNTS THE WORLD WILL BURN NO CITIES NOW. HIS KHALASAR SHALL TRAMPLE NO NATIONS INTO DUST.
I SPOKE FOR YOU. I **SAVED** YOU!
THREE RIDERS HAD TAKEN ME AND THE FOURTH WAS IN ME WHEN YOU RODE PAST.
I SAW MY GOD'S HOUSE BURN, I HEARD CHILDREN CRYING AS YOUR RIDERS DROVE THEM WITH WHIPS.
TELL ME THEN WHAT YOU **SAVED**.
YOUR LIFE!
SEE, KHALEESI, WHAT LIFE IS WORTH WHEN ALL THE REST IS GONE.
TAKE HER! BIND HER!

THEY LED KHAL DROGO BACK TO THE TENT.
A WORD, AND DANY COULD HAVE THE MAEGI'S HEAD, YET THEN WHAT WOULD SHE HAVE? A HEAD?

IF LIFE WAS WORTHLESS, WHAT WAS DEATH?

IT WAS WELL PAST DARK BEFORE SHE WAS DONE, BUT SHE HAD SLEPT ENOUGH.
TOO LONG.

SHE LED HIM OUTSIDE. THE DOTHRAKI BELIEVED ALL THINGS OF IMPORTANCE MUST BE DONE UNDER AN OPEN SKY.
REMEMBER, DROGO. THE DAY WE WED.

REMEMBER AND COME BACK TO ME.
YET DROGO DID NOT FEEL OR SPEAK OR RISE.
WHEN THE SUN RISES IN THE WEST AND SETS IN THE EAST.

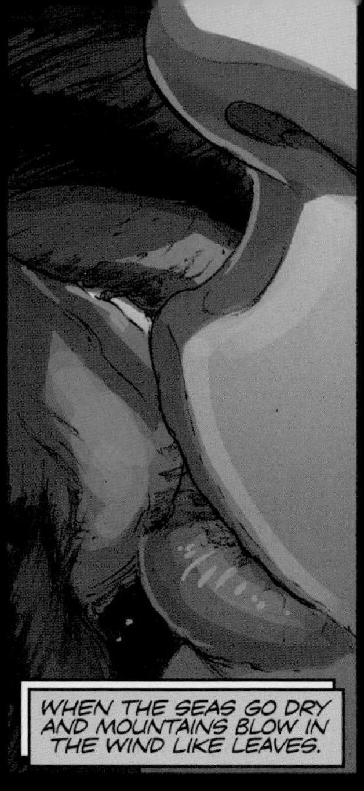
WHEN THE SEAS GO DRY AND MOUNTAINS BLOW IN THE WIND LIKE LEAVES.

WHEN HER WOMB QUICKENED AGAIN AND SHE BORE A LIVING CHILD. **THEN** HE WOULD RETURN.
NEVER, THE DARKNESS CRIED. NEVER, NEVER, NEVER...

SHE PRESSED THE CUSHION DOWN ACROSS HIS FACE.

ISSUE #24

JON, PLEASE! YOU MUST NOT DO THIS!
GHOST. TO ME.
YOU CAN'T! I... I WON'T LET YOU.
I WOULD SOONER NOT HURT YOU. MOVE ASIDE, SAM, OR I'LL RIDE YOU DOWN.
YOU WON'T. YOU HAVE TO LISTEN TO ME–
JON PUT SPURS TO HORSEFLESH. FOR A MOMENT, SAMWELL TARLY STOOD HIS GROUND.
THEN HE JUMPED ASIDE, AS JON HAD KNOWN HE WOULD.

HE NEEDED TO GET AS FAR FROM THE WALL AS HE COULD BEFORE THEY REALIZED HE WAS GONE. ON THE MORROW, HE WOULD STRIKE OUT OVERLAND TO THROW OFF PURSUIT, BUT SPEED WAS MORE IMPORTANT THAN DECEPTION.
THEY WOULD KNOW WHERE HE WAS GOING.
EVEN NOW, HE DID NOT KNOW IF HE WAS DOING THE HONORABLE THING. SOUTHRONS HAD THEIR SEPTONS TO HELP SORT OUT RIGHT FROM WRONG.
BUT THE STARKS WORSHIPPED THE OLD GODS. AND IF THE HEART TREES HEARD, THEY DID NOT SPEAK.
JON WAS WHO HE WAS. BASTARD, OATHBREAKER, MOTHERLESS, FRIENDLESS, AND DAMNED.
BUT NO MATTER—SO LONG AS HE LIVED LONG ENOUGH TO STAND AT HIS BROTHER'S SIDE AND AVENGE THEIR FATHER.
HE TRIED TO IMAGINE ROBB'S GREETING, BUT HE COULD NOT. INSTEAD, HE FOUND HIMSELF THINKING OF THE DESERTER HIS FATHER HAD BEHEADED.
HE WONDERED WHAT LORD EDDARD MIGHT HAVE DONE IF THE DESERTER HAD BEEN HIS BROTHER BENJEN INSTEAD OF A STRANGER.
SURELY ROBB WOULD WELCOME HIM. OR ELSE...
HE RACED AS IF TO OUTRUN HIS DOUBTS. GHOST KEPT CLOSE FOR HALF A MILE, THEN VANISHED BEHIND.
HE WOULD FOLLOW AT HIS OWN PACE.

SCATTERED LIGHTS FLICKERED THROUGH THE TREES ON BOTH SIDES OF THE ROAD. MOLE TOWN.
MOST OF THE VILLAGE WAS UNDER GROUND, WARM CELLARS CONNECTED BY TUNNELS. ON THE SURFACE, ALL WAS STILL.
STILL HE DID NOT PAUSE TO REST UNTIL HE WAS WELL PAST IT. FOR HALF AN HOUR, HE WALKED HIS MARE DOWN SIDE PATHS BESIDE THE MAIN ROAD, BUT IT BROUGHT HIM LITTLE PEACE.
I AM DOING THE RIGHT THING, HE TOLD HIMSELF. SO WHY DO I FEEL SO BAD?
IT HAD BEEN HARD TO ABANDON LONGCLAW, BUT JON WAS NOT SO LOST TO HONOR AS TO TAKE THE SWORD WITH HIM.
CHAK
GHOST?
NO, NOT GHOST.
RIDERS, FROM THE NORTH.

—CERTAIN HE CAME THIS WAY?
HE COULD HAVE RIDDEN EAST. OR CUT THROUGH THE WOODS.
IN THE DARK? IF YOU DIDN'T FALL OFF YOUR HORSE, YOU'D GET LOST.
I WOULD NOT GET LOST. YOU CAN TELL SOUTH BY THE STARS.
KEEP QUIET! I THOUGHT I HEARD SOMETHING.
I THOUGHT I HEARD A HORSE.
THERE'S NOTHING *THERE*.
HHINNIE
THERE!
I HEARD IT TOO!
JON!

STOP! YOU CAN'T OUTRUN US!
GET BACK! I DON'T WISH TO HURT YOU, BUT I WILL IF I MUST.
ONE AGAINST FOUR?
WHAT DO YOU WANT FROM ME?
WE WANT TO TAKE YOU BACK WHERE YOU BELONG.
THEY'LL CUT OFF YOUR HEAD IF THEY CATCH YOU.
DON'T YOU UNDERSTAND? THEY MURDERED MY FATHER.
MY BROTHER ROBB IS FIGHTING IN THE RIVERLANDS—
WE'RE SORRY ABOUT YOUR FATHER, BUT IT DOESN'T MATTER. ONCE YOU SAY THE WORDS, YOU CAN'T LEAVE, NO MATTER WHAT.
AND YOU SAID THE WORDS.
NOW MY WATCH BEGINS. IT SHALL NOT END UNTIL MY DEATH.
I SHALL LIVE AND DIE AT MY POST.

YOU DON'T HAVE TO TELL ME THE WORDS. I KNOW THEM AS WELL AS YOU.
THEY WEREN'T EVEN WEARING ARMOR. HE COULD CUT THEM TO PIECES.
I AM THE SWORD IN THE DARKNESS. THE WATCHER ON THE WALLS.
I AM THE FIRE THAT BURNS AGAINST THE COLD, THE LIGHT THAT BRINGS THE DAWN.

THE HORN THAT WAKES THE SLEEPERS. THE SHIELD THAT GUARDS THE REALMS OF MEN.
I PLEDGE MY LIFE AND HONOR TO THE NIGHT'S WATCH FOR THIS NIGHT...

...AND ALL THE NIGHTS TO COME.
SO HERE ARE YOUR CHOICES. KILL ME, OR COME BACK WITH ME.

DAMN YOU ALL.

WE'D BETTER HURRY. IF WE'RE NOT BACK BY FIRST LIGHT, THE OLD BEAR WILL HAVE ALL OUR HEADS.
THE RIDE BACK SEEMED SHORTER THAN THE JOURNEY SOUTH. PERHAPS BECAUSE HIS MIND WAS ELSEWHERE.
THEY COULD TAKE HIM BACK, BUT THEY COULD NOT MAKE HIM STAY.
DAWN WAS STILL AN HOUR OFF WHEN THEY REACHED CASTLE BLACK. IT DID NOT SEEM LIKE HOME.
GIVE US A HAND WITH THE HORSES, SAM.
WE'VE A LONG DAY AHEAD AND NO SLEEP TO FACE IT ON, THANKS TO LORD SNOW.
I— I'M GLAD THEY FOUND YOU.
I'M NOT.

JON WENT TO THE KITCHENS AS HE DID EVERY MORNING, AND THEN TO THE LORD COMMANDER.
PUT THE FOOD ON THE TABLE.
CORN! CORN!

THE THINGS WE LOVE DESTROY US, LAD. REMEMBER WHEN I TOLD YOU THAT?
I REMEMBER.

DOUBTLESS YOU LOVED YOUR FATHER.
YOU LOOK WEARY. WAS YOUR MOONLIGHT RIDE SO TIRING?

YOU KNOW?
KNOW! KNOW!

DO YOU THINK I BECAME LORD COMMANDER BY BEING DUMB AS A STUMP? HONOR SET YOU ON THE KINGSROAD. AND HONOR BROUGHT YOU BACK.
MY FRIENDS BROUGHT ME BACK.

DID I SAY IT WAS **YOUR** HONOR?

THEY KILLED MY FATHER. DID YOU EXPECT ME TO DO NOTHING?
I EXPECTED YOU TO DO AS YOU DID. IF YOUR BROTHERS HAD NOT FETCHED YOU BACK, YOU WOULD HAVE BEEN TAKEN ALONG THE WAY. AND NOT BY FRIENDS.
I KNOW THE PENALTY FOR DESERTION. I AM NOT AFRAID TO DIE.
NOR LIVE, I HOPE. YOU HAVE NOT DESERTED... YET.
DO YOU THINK YOU CAN BRING YOUR FATHER BACK? WE'VE **SEEN** THE DEAD COME BACK, YOU AND ME.
AND YOUR BROTHER HAS THE POWER OF THE NORTH BEHIND HIM. WHY DO YOU IMAGINE THEY NEED **YOUR** HELP?
THE COLD WINDS ARE RISING, SNOW. RANGERS FROM THE SHADOW TOWER HAVE FOUND WHOLE VILLAGES ABANDONED.
QUORIN HALFHAND TOOK A CAPTIVE WHO SWEARS MANCE RAYDER IS MASSING ALL HIS PEOPLE— THOUGH TO WHAT END THE GODS ALONE KNOW.

DO YOU THINK YOUR UNCLE BENJEN WAS THE ONLY RANGER WE LOST THIS YEAR? DO YOU THINK YOUR BROTHER'S WAR IS MORE IMPORTANT THAN OURS?
...NO.

THE BLOOD OF THE FIRST MEN FLOWS IN YOUR VEINS, THE MEN WHO **BUILT** THE WALL. I THINK YOU WERE MEANT TO BE HERE.
AND I WANT YOU AND THAT WOLF OF YOURS WITH US WHEN WE GO BEYOND THE WALL.

BEYOND THE WALL?

I MEAN TO FIND BEN STARK, ALIVE OR DEAD. BUT I DO NOT CARE TO WAKE EVERY MORNING WONDERING IF YOU'VE RUN OFF.

I AM... YOURS, MY LORD. I WILL NOT RUN AGAIN.
FORGIVE ME, FATHER, HE THOUGHT. ***ROBB, ARYA, BRAN.*** *I CANNOT HELP YOU.*
THIS IS MY PLACE.

GOOD. NOW GO PUT ON YOUR SWORD.

IT SEEMED A THOUSAND YEARS AGO THAT CATELYN HAD CARRIED HER INFANT SON OUT OF RIVERRUN TO BEGIN THEIR JOURNEY TO WINTERFELL.
AND AS THEY RETURNED, THE BOY WORE PLATE AND MAIL IN PLACE OF SWADDLING CLOTHES.
THEY PASSED THROUGH THE PORTCULLIS OF THE WATER GATE. SHE WONDERED HOW DEEP THE RUST WENT, AND HOW WELL IT WOULD STAND UP TO A RAM.
THOUGHTS LIKE THAT WERE SELDOM FAR FROM HER MIND THESE DAYS.
FROM THE RAMPARTS, THEY SHOUTED DOWN HER NAME AND ROBB'S AND WINTERFELL. YET IT DID NOT LIFT HER HEART.
BRING THEM IN!
OH, NED...SHE WONDERED IF HER HEART WOULD EVER LIFT AGAIN.
SWEET SISTER. WHEN WE HEARD ABOUT LORD EDDARD...I SWEAR, YOU WILL HAVE VENGEANCE.

YES, EDMURE? AND WILL THAT BRING NED BACK TO ME?
I MUST SEE FATHER.

HE IS IN HIS SOLAR. HE WANTED TO SEE YOU AT ONCE.

HE IS BEDRIDDEN.
HOW BAD IS HE?

THE PAIN IS CONSTANT. AND GRIEVOUS. HE WILL NOT BE WITH US LONG.

YOU SHOULD HAVE SENT WORD.
HE FORBADE IT. IF THE LANNISTERS HAD KNOWN HOW FRAIL HE WAS...

...THEY MIGHT ATTACK?
IT WAS HER FAULT. ALL OF IT. IF ONLY SHE HAD NOT TAKEN IT UPON HERSELF TO SEIZE THE DWARF.

LITTLE CAT? MY LITTLE CAT. I WATCHED FOR YOU...
HOSTER TULLY HAD ALWAYS BEEN A BIG MAN. TALL AND BROAD IN HIS YOUTH, PORTLY AS HE GOT OLDER.

THE LAST TIME SHE HAD SEEN HIM, HIS HAIR AND BEARD HAD BEEN BROWN STREAKED WITH GREY.
YOU SHOULD HAVE TOLD ME. A RIDER. A RAVEN—
RIDERS ARE TAKEN. RAVENS ARE BROUGHT DOWN.

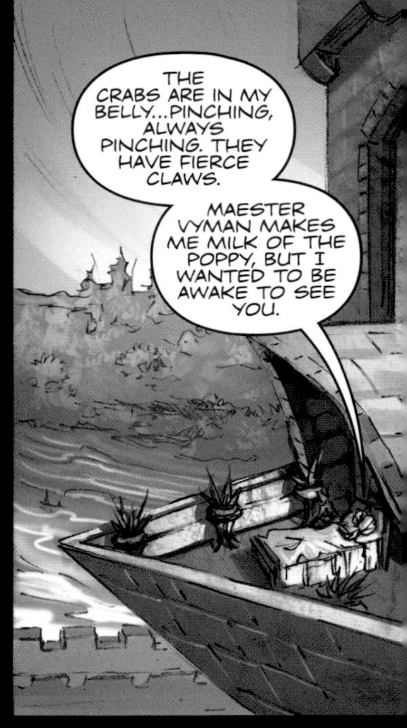
THE CRABS ARE IN MY BELLY...PINCHING, ALWAYS PINCHING. THEY HAVE FIERCE CLAWS.
MAESTER VYMAN MAKES ME MILK OF THE POPPY, BUT I WANTED TO BE AWAKE TO SEE YOU.

I'M HERE, FATHER. WITH ROBB, MY SON. WE'VE BROUGHT YOU JAIME LANNISTER IN IRONS.
AND BRYNDEN. YOUR BROTHER IS HERE AS WELL, MY LORD.

THE BLACKFISH RETURNED FROM THE VALE? AND LYSA AS WELL?
NO. SHE IS WITH HER SON IN THE EYRIE.

ROBB WILL BE WAITING. WILL YOU SEE HIM? AND BRYNDEN?
YOUR SON...YES...I REMEMBER WHEN HE WAS BORN...
HAS THE BLACKFISH WED YET? TAKEN SOME...GIRL TO WIFE?
EVEN ON HIS DEATHBED, CATELYN THOUGHT SADLY.
YOU KNOW HE HAS NOT, FATHER. NOR WILL HE EVER.
I COMMANDED HIM! I WAS HIS LORD. MY RIGHT, TO MAKE HIS MATCH.
REDWYNE... PRETTY GIRL...
FRECKLES.
BETHANY REDWYNE WED LORD ROWAN YEARS AGO. SHE HAS THREE CHILDREN BY HIM.
EVEN SO... HAS HE WED ANYONE? SEND HIM LATER. I'LL SLEEP NOW.

SHE FOUND ROBB BEFORE THE HEART TREE WITH THE OTHERS WHO KEPT THE OLD GODS. SHE DID NOT DISTURB THEM.
THE GODS MUST HAVE THEIR DUE. EVEN CRUEL GODS WHO WOULD TAKE NED FROM HER. AND HER FATHER.
MOTHER. WE MUST CALL A COUNCIL. THERE ARE THINGS TO BE DECIDED.
YOUR GRANDFATHER WOULD LIKE TO SEE YOU. ROBB, HE'S VERY SICK.
I AM SORRY, MOTHER—FOR LORD HOSTER AND FOR YOU—BUT FIRST WE MUST MEET. WE'VE HAD WORD FROM THE SOUTH.
RENLY BARATHEON HAS CLAIMED HIS BROTHER'S CROWN.
RENLY? I HAD THOUGHT IT WOULD BE LORD STANNIS—
SO DID WE ALL, MY LADY.

THE ARGUING RAGED ON LATE INTO THE NIGHT. EACH LORD HAD THE RIGHT TO SPEAK, AND SPEAK THEY DID.
AND SHOUT, AND CURSE, AND REASON, AND CAJOLE, AND JEST, AND BARGAIN.
MANY WANTED TO MARCH ON HARRENHALL AT ONCE TO MEET LORD TYWIN. OTHERS COUNSELED PATIENCE. WHAT ONE URGED, ANOTHER OPPOSED. LORD JONOS BRACKEN EVEN ROSE TO INSIST THEY PLEDGE THEIR FEALTY TO KING RENLY AND MOVE SOUTH TO JOIN HIM.
IT WAS ONLY THEN THAT ROBB SPOKE.
RENLY IS NOT THE KING.
YOU CANNOT MEAN TO HOLD TO JOFFREY. HE PUT YOUR FATHER TO THE SWORD!
THAT MAKES HIM EVIL, BUT I DO NOT KNOW THAT IT MAKES RENLY KING.

LORD STANNIS HAS THE BETTER CLAIM.
BUT RENLY IS CROWNED. WITH WINTERFELL AND RIVERRUN, HE WILL HAVE FIVE OF THE SEVEN GREAT HOUSES. SIX, IF THE ARRYNS BESTIR THEMSELVES.
WHAT DOES LORD STANNIS HAVE AGAINST THAT?

THE *RIGHT*.

THE LANNISTERS KILLED MY FATHER FOR A TRAITOR. THAT WAS A LIE, BUT IF JOFFREY IS THE RIGHTFUL KING AND WE FIGHT AGAINST HIM, ***WE*** WILL BE TRAITORS.

LET THESE TWO KINGS PLAY THEIR GAME OF THRONES. WITH RENLY ARMING, LORD TYWIN WOULD WELCOME A TRUCE AND THE RANSOM FOR HIS SON–
CRAVEN!
BEGGING TRUCE WOULD MAKE US SEEM WEAK!
RANSOMS BE DAMNED, WE MUST NOT GIVE UP THE KINGSLAYER!

WHY NOT A ***PEACE?***

LORD EDDARD WAS YOUR LIEGE. I SHARED HIS BED AND BORE HIS CHILDREN. DO YOU THINK I LOVED HIM LESS THAN YOU? BUT HE IS GONE.
NOW I MUST THINK OF THE LIVING. MY DAUGHTERS BACK FROM KING'S LANDING. MY SON RULING WINTERFELL FROM HIS FATHER'S SEAT.
I WANT AN END TO THIS.

PEACE IS SWEET, MY LADY. BUT ON WHAT TERMS?
WHAT DID TORRHEN AND MY EDDARD DIE FOR, IF I AM TO GO BACK WITH NOTHING BUT THEIR BONES?
GREGOR CLEGANE LAID WASTE TO MY FIELDS AND SLAUGHTERED MY SMALLFOLK. AM I TO BEND THE KNEE TO THE ONES WHO SENT HIM?
IF WE MAKE PEACE WITH JOFFREY, ARE WE NOT TRAITORS TO KING RENLY? AND IF THE STAG PREVAILS AGAINST THE LION, WHERE WOULD THAT LEAVE US?
WHATEVER YOU MAY DECIDE FOR YOURSELVES, I SHALL NEVER CALL A LANNISTER MY KING!
NOR I!
I NEVER WILL.
THEY HAD ALMOST LISTENED, ALMOST... BUT THE MOMENT WAS GONE.
THERE WOULD BE NO PEACE, NO CHANCE TO HEAL, NO SAFETY.
MY LORDS! RENLY BARATHEON IS NOTHING TO ME. NOR STANNIS NEITHER!

WHY SHOULD THEY RULE OVER ME AND MINE FROM HIGHGARDEN OR DORNE? WHAT DO THEY KNOW OF THE WALL OR THE BARROWS OF THE FIRST MEN?
IT WAS THE DRAGONS WE MARRIED, AND THE DRAGONS ARE DEAD!

THERE'S THE ONLY KING I'LL BEND MY KNEE TO. THE KING IN THE NORTH!
I'LL HAVE PEACE ON THOSE TERMS.

THE KING OF WINTER!

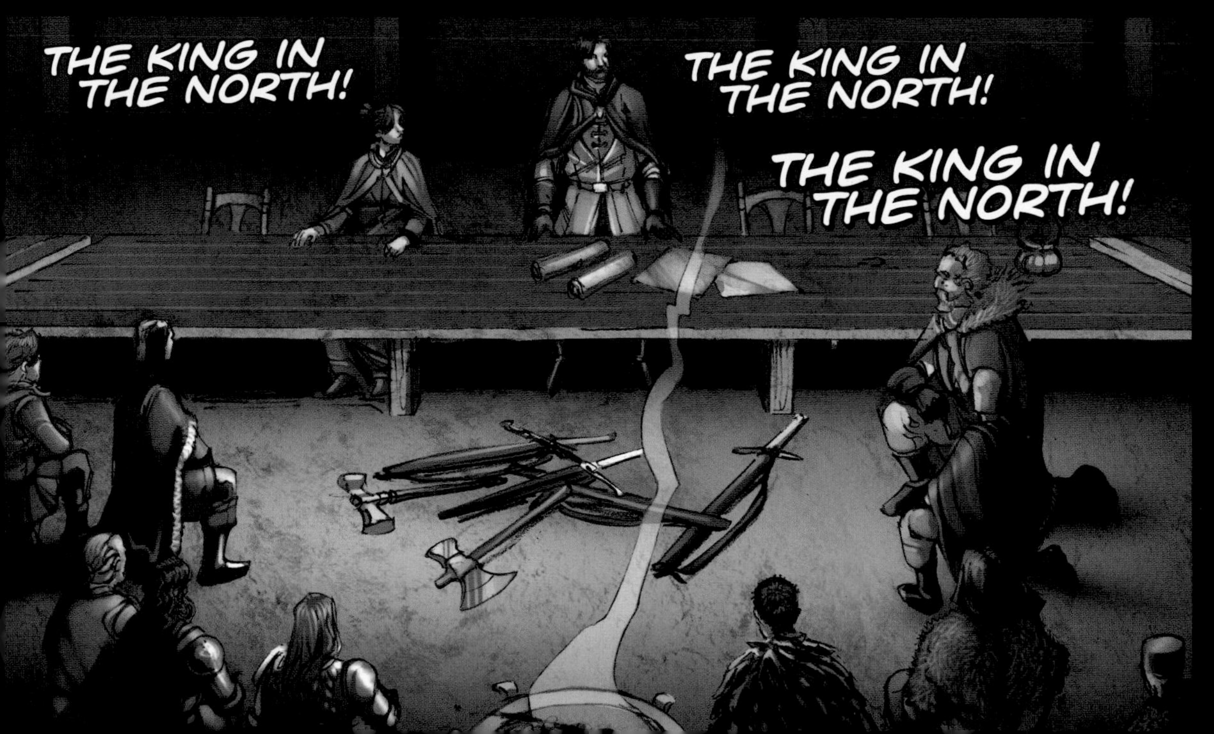
THE KING IN THE NORTH!
THE KING IN THE NORTH!
THE KING IN THE NORTH!

RAKHARO HAD CHOSEN THE STALLION FROM THE SMALL HERD THAT REMAINED TO THEM. IT WAS NOT THE EQUAL OF KHAL DROGO'S RED, BUT FEW WERE.
IT'S NOT ENOUGH TO KILL A HORSE. THE BLOOD BY ITSELF IS NOTHING.
WHATEVER YOU MEAN TO DO, IT WILL NOT WORK. LOOSE THESE BONDS, AND I WILL HELP YOU.
JHOGO! I AM TIRED OF THE MAEGI'S BRAYING.

THE LAND WAS DEAD AND PARCHED. GOOD WOOD WAS HARD TO COME BY.
HER FORAGERS HAD RETURNED WITH GNARLED COTTONWOOD AND SHEAVES OF BROWN GRASS.

ON THE PLATFORM, THEY PILED DROGO'S PAINTED VESTS, HIS SADDLES AND HARNESS, THE WHIP HIS FATHER HAD GIVEN HIM. HIS TREASURES.
AGGO WOULD HAVE ADDED THE WEAPONS DROGO'S BLOODRIDERS HAD GIVEN DANY, BUT SHE FORBADE IT. THOSE WERE HERS.

PRINCESS–
WHY DO YOU CALL ME THAT? MY BROTHER WAS YOUR KING, WAS HE NOT? I AM HIS HEIR, THE LAST BLOOD OF HOUSE TARGARYEN.
MY... QUEEN.

MY SWORD IS YOURS AS IT WAS HIS, BUT ALSO MY HEART. I AM ONLY A KNIGHT, AND I HAVE NOTHING TO OFFER YOU BUT EXILE, BUT I BEG YOU, HEAR ME.
LET KHAL DROGO GO.

COME EAST WITH ME. YI TI. QARTH. ASSHAI BY THE SHADOW. WE WILL SEE ALL THE WONDERS YET UNSEEN, AND DRINK WHAT WINES THE GODS SEE FIT TO SERVE US.
PLEASE, KHALEESI. I KNOW WHAT YOU INTEND. DO NOT.

I MUST. YOU DO NOT UNDERSTAND.

YOU ARE MY QUEEN AND MY SWORD IS YOURS, BUT DO NOT ASK ME TO STAND ASIDE AS YOU CLIMB ON DROGO'S PYRE. I WILL NOT WATCH YOU BURN.
IS THAT WHAT YOU FEAR? I AM NOT SUCH A CHILD AS THAT, SWEET SER.

YOU DO NOT MEAN TO DIE WITH HIM? YOU SWEAR IT, MY QUEEN?
I SWEAR IT.

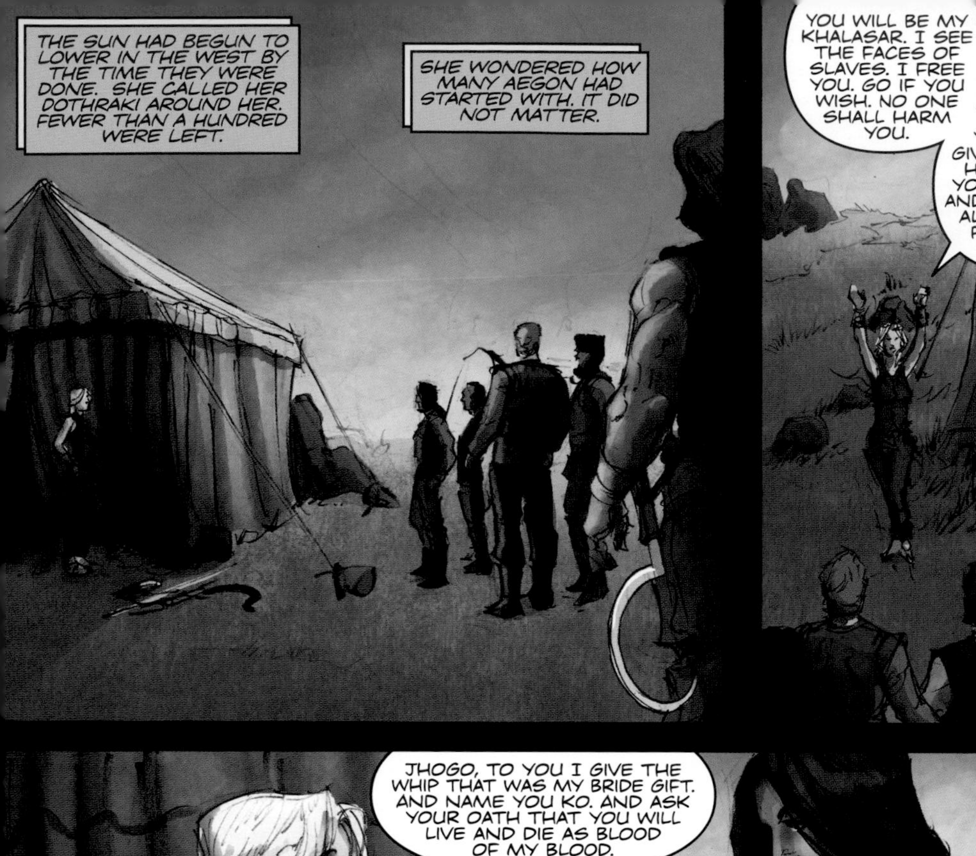
THE SUN HAD BEGUN TO LOWER IN THE WEST BY THE TIME THEY WERE DONE. SHE CALLED HER DOTHRAKI AROUND HER. FEWER THAN A HUNDRED WERE LEFT.
SHE WONDERED HOW MANY AEGON HAD STARTED WITH. IT DID NOT MATTER.
YOU WILL BE MY KHALASAR. I SEE THE FACES OF SLAVES. I FREE YOU. GO IF YOU WISH. NO ONE SHALL HARM YOU.
IF YOU STAY, GIVE ME YOUR HANDS AND YOUR HEARTS, AND THERE WILL ALWAYS BE A PLACE FOR YOU.

JHOGO, TO YOU I GIVE THE WHIP THAT WAS MY BRIDE GIFT. AND NAME YOU KO. AND ASK YOUR OATH THAT YOU WILL LIVE AND DIE AS BLOOD OF MY BLOOD.

KHALEESI, THIS IS NOT DONE. IT WOULD SHAME ME TO BE BLOODRIDER TO A WOMAN.
IF I LOOK BACK, SHE THOUGHT, I AM LOST.

AGGO, TO YOU I GIVE THE DRAGONBONE BOW THAT WAS MY BRIDE GIFT, AND NAME YOU KO, AND ASK YOUR OATH THAT YOU WILL LIVE AND DIE AS BLOOD OF MY BLOOD.
I CANNOT SAY THESE WORDS. ONLY A MAN CAN LEAD A KHALASAR OR NAME A KO.

RAKHARO, YOU SHALL HAVE THE ARAKH THAT WAS MY BRIDE GIFT, AND YOU TOO I NAME MY KO AND ASK THAT YOU LIVE AND DIE AS BLOOD OF MY BLOOD.
YOU ARE KHALEESI. I SHALL RIDE WITH YOU TO VAES DOTHRAK AND KEEP YOU SAFE FROM HARM UNTIL YOU JOIN THE DOSH KHALEEN. NO MORE CAN I PROMISE.

SER JORAH MORMONT, FIRST AND GREATEST OF MY KNIGHTS. I HAVE NO BRIDE GIFT TO GIVE YOU, BUT I SWEAR THAT ONE DAY YOU SHALL HAVE FROM MY HANDS A LONGSWORD LIKE NONE THE WORLD HAS EVER SEEN.
DRAGON-FORGED AND MADE OF VALYRIAN STEEL.
AND I ASK YOUR OATH.
YOU HAVE IT MY QUEEN. I VOW TO SERVE YOU OBEY YOU, AND DIE FOR YOU IF NEED BE.
WHATEVER MAY COME?
WHATEVER MAY COME.
I SHALL HOLD YOU TO THAT OATH. I PRAY YOU NEVER REGRET THE GIVING OF IT.
YOU ARE FIRST OF MY QUEENSGUARD.

THE DOTHRAKI WERE MUTTERING AND GIVING HER STRANGE LOOKS. THEY THOUGHT HER MAD. AND PERHAPS SHE WAS.
IF I LOOK BACK, I AM LOST.
HER BATH WAS SCALDING HOT, BUT SHE DID NOT FLINCH OR CRY OUT. SHE LIKED THE HEAT.
WHEN SHE WAS CLEAN, SHE SENT HER HANDMAIDS AWAY SO THAT SHE MIGHT PREPARE KHAL DROGO FOR HIS RIDE INTO THE NIGHT LANDS.
SHE WASHED HIS BODY CLEAN AND BRUSHED AND OILED HIS HAIR, RUNNING HER FINGERS THROUGH IT FOR THE LAST TIME.
HE SMELLED LIKE GRASS AND WARM EARTH, LIKE SMOKE AND SEMEN AND HORSES. HE SMELLED LIKE DROGO.
FORGIVE ME, SUN OF MY LIFE, SHE THOUGHT. FORGIVE ME FOR ALL I HAVE DONE AND ALL I MUST DO. I PAID THE PRICE, BUT IT WAS TOO HIGH. TOO HIGH...

IRRI! BRING MY EGGS.
THEY BROUGHT HIM FORTH AND POURED OIL OVER THE PYRE, SOAKING THE SILKS AND THE BRUSH AND THE BUNDLES OF DRY GRASS.
MY QUEEN, DROGO WILL HAVE NO USE FOR DRAGON'S EGGS IN THE NIGHT LAND. BETTER TO SELL THEM IN ASSHAI. THEY WILL MAKE YOU A WEALTHY WOMAN TO THE END OF YOUR DAYS.
THEY WERE NOT GIVEN TO ME TO SELL.
SHE CLIMBED THE PYRE HERSELF TO PLACE THEM. WHEN SHE KISSED DROGO FOR THE LAST TIME, SHE TASTED THE SWEETNESS OF OIL ON HIS LIPS.
YOU ARE MAD!
IS IT SO FAR FROM MADNESS TO WISDOM?
SER JORAH, TAKE THIS MAEGI AND BIND HER TO THE PYRE.
TO THE... MY QUEEN, NO, HEAR ME—
YOU SWORE TO OBEY ME. WHATEVER MAY COME.

I THANK YOU, MIRRI MAZ DUUR, FOR THE LESSONS YOU HAVE TAUGHT ME.
YOU WILL NOT HEAR ME SCREAM.
I WILL, BUT IT IS NOT YOUR SCREAMS I WANT. ONLY YOUR LIFE.
I REMEMBER WHAT YOU TOLD ME. ONLY DEATH CAN PAY FOR LIFE.
THE CONTEMPT WAS GONE FROM THE MAEGI'S FLAT BLACK EYES. IN ITS PLACE WAS SOMETHING THAT MIGHT HAVE BEEN FEAR.
WHEN A HORSELORD DIES, HIS HORSE IS SLAIN WITH HIM SO THAT HE MIGHT RIDE PROUD INTO THE NIGHT LANDS. THE MORE FIERCELY THE MAN FOUGHT IN LIFE, THE BRIGHTER HIS STAR WOULD SHINE.
THERE WAS NOTHING TO BE DONE NOW BUT WATCH FOR THE FIRST STAR.
THERE!
THE FIRST STAR WAS A COMET, BURNING RED. THE DRAGON'S TAIL. SHE COULD NOT HAVE ASKED FOR A STRONGER SIGN.
THE OIL TOOK FIRE AT ONCE.
THE BRUSH AND DRIED GRASS, A HEARTBEAT LATER.

THE PYRE ROARED IN THE DUSK LIKE A GREAT BEAST, DROWNING OUT MIRRI MAZ DUUR'S SCREAMS.
DANY COULD SMELL THE ODOR OF BURNING FLESH, NO DIFFERENT THAN HORSEFLESH ROASTING IN A FIREPIT.
THE FLAMES REACHED HER DROGO, AND NOW THEY WERE ALL AROUND HIM.
HUGE GOUTS OF FIRE UNFURLED THEIR BANNERS IN THAT HELLISH WIND, GLOWING CINDERS RISING ON THE SMOKE LIKE SO MANY NEWBORN FIREFLIES.
THE HEAT DROVE THE DOTHRAKI BACK, BUT DANY STOOD HER GROUND. SHE WAS THE BLOOD OF THE DRAGON, AND THE FIRE WAS IN HER.
SHE HAD SENSED THE TRUTH OF IT LONG AGO.
ANOTHER STEP, AND DANY COULD FEEL THE HEAT OF THE SAND ON THE SOLES OF HER FEET. THE FLAMES WERE SO BEAUTIFUL. THE LOVELIEST THINGS SHE HAD EVER SEEN.

HER VEST BEGAN TO SMOLDER, SO DANY SHRUGGED IT OFF.
SHE SAW CRIMSON FIRELIONS AND GREAT YELLOW SERPENTS AND UNICORNS MADE OF PALE BLUE FLAME.
FOR AN INSTANT, SHE GLIMPSED KHAL DROGO BEFORE HER, MOUNTED ON HIS SMOKY STALLION, A FLAMING WHIP IN HIS HAND.
HE SMILED, AND THE WHIP SNAKED DOWN AT THE PYRE.
SHE HEARD A CRACK. THE SHATTERING OF STONE.
ONLY DEATH CAN PAY FOR LIFE.
SER JORAH WAS SHOUTING BEHIND HER, BUT THAT DID NOT MATTER ANYMORE.
ONLY THE FIRE MATTERED.
DO NOT FEAR FOR ME, MY GOOD KNIGHT. THE FIRE IS MINE. I AM DAENERYS STORMBORN, DAUGHTER OF DRAGONS, BRIDE OF DRAGONS, MOTHER OF DRAGONS.
DON'T YOU SEE?
THERE WAS A SECOND CRACK, LOUD AND SHARP AS THUNDER.
THE THIRD WAS AS LOUD AND SHARP AS THE BREAKING OF THE WORLD.

WHEN THE FIRE DIED AT LAST AND THE GROUND BECAME COOL ENOUGH TO WALK UPON, SER JORAH FOUND HER.
MY QUEEN...
THE MEN OF THE KHAS CAME UP BEHIND HIM. AND AFTER THEM, HER HANDMAIDS. AND THEN ALL THE OTHER DOTHRAKI.
BLOOD OF MY BLOOD.
BLOOD OF MY BLOOD.
BLOOD OF MY BLOOD.
THEY WERE HERS NOW—HERS AS THEY HAD NEVER BEEN DROGO'S.

AND FOR THE FIRST TIME IN HUNDREDS OF YEARS, THE NIGHT CAME ALIVE WITH THE MUSIC OF DRAGONS.

AND NOW...
HERE IS A SPECIAL INSIDER'S LOOK AT

THE MAKING OF

A GAME OF THRONES

THE GRAPHIC NOVEL
VOLUME 4

WITH COMMENTARY BY
ANNE GROELL (SERIES EDITOR)
TOMMY PATTERSON (ARTIST)

THE FINAL VOLUME BY ANNE GROELL

Well, this is it. We have reached the end of the epic graphic journey that was *A Game of Thrones: The Graphic Novel.* And it has been a long one in the making. We acquired graphic rights to the novel in early 2010, then spent the rest of 2010 lining up the talent and confirming our partnership agreements. The first issue was assembled in April of 2011, and the last one put to bed in January of 2015. So we have all been living inside *A Game of Thrones* for a long time now. We had a lot of fun over the almost four years of the run (although there were a fair number of headaches), and we all learned a lot. And we all remain very proud of the product we created.

But now that we are at the end, I wanted to let Tommy Patterson—whose vision of Westeros and the lands beyond has sprung so vividly to life on these pages over the years—have the final word. So I will now turn the pages over to him, to tell you a bit about the art of creating and drawing six of his main characters.

So without further ado . . . Tommy Patterson!

BRINGING CHARACTERS TO LIFE BY TOMMY PATTERSON

We've come to the end, my friends. The final graphic hardcover of the first book of *A Song of Ice and Fire: A Game of Thrones*! I was given a couple of choices for this wrap-up and decided to offer something that might set you on your own path, and perhaps inspire you to pick up your own tool of choice and create art!

One of the things I've learned in my years of being an artist is that everyone *wants* to draw (or paint or sculpt or even make music), but hasn't been told that they could. It's as if everyone is waiting for permission. Of course, some just say, "I can't!" Well, that doesn't fly with me. You can . . . and you should!

I'll do my best in the next few pages to inspire and provide a framework for autodidactic learning. So let's revisit my previous paragraph and explore that permission problem. Modern methods of teaching focus on input and verbatim output. Bah! We want creativity! I much prefer the original seven liberal arts, also known as the Trivium and the Quadrivium. I implore you to research this classical method of learning.

The Trivium consists of:

- GRAMMAR: This answers the Who, What, Where, and When of a subject.
- LOGIC: This answers the Why of a subject.
- RHETORIC: This provides the How of a subject.

The Quadrivium consists of:
- ARITHMETIC: Numbers in themselves, which are a pure abstraction—that is, outside of space and time.
- GEOMETRY: Numbers in space.
- MUSIC OR HARMONIC THEORY: Numbers in time.
- ASTRONOMY: Numbers in space and time.

When you are learning how to draw, you need to learn in the correct order. If you have a method, the hours spent practicing will be more efficient. So the ten-thousand-hour rule can get out of our face! We can achieve our goal in no time by using the proper methods.

Grammar comes first: things such as anatomy, perspective, construction, and hierarchy. Once you understand basics, you can move to more advanced concepts such as color, shape, form, and texture. Trust me, there is no end to learning, and that keeps you fresh and on your toes.

Logic comes next. This is the self-critique. Here we ask: Why? Why is this the right pose? Why am I choosing a specific angle? Simply having the grammar of what to draw doesn't mean the drawing will make sense. In the logic phase, you eliminate the contradictions. If the character is supposed to be angry, drawing a static expression doesn't convey the emotion you are trying to get across. So erase it and try again!

Rhetoric is the individuality you bring to the drawing once you've learned grammar and eliminated the contradictions with logic. Rhetoric is your voice and creativity. Your life's experiences are what provide the lens, the particularity, that makes it a piece only you can create.

So how do I go about drawing the *A Game of Thrones* characters? For myself, when reading the character descriptions in the book, I begin to develop an image based on the grammar provided, and my experiences then help me to construct an image of that character. For example, I drew on the sorrow-filled people in my past for Jon Snow, and on the snobby bitches I've had contact with for Cersei. With that method, it's kind of easy to make the characters distinct. George is successful because his vision comes across extremely well to the reader. He doesn't describe a chicken leg; he describes the peppered crust and juicy meat. *A Game of Thrones* and the other books in the series are very visceral. So I wanted to make sure my drawings conveyed that same reality.

I hope the following pages will give you some insight into my mind-set while drawing the characters.

For starters, my method of constructing the drawing is the same for all the characters. I start by roughing out the basic shapes of the head with the side of my pencil. It's a mind hack, so I don't commit too early and waste time drawing details. The details I save until the end of the drawing. I use rudimentary shapes like spheres, pyramids, and cylinders early in the drawing process. (See Figure 1)

FIGURE 1

I then find lines, with the point of the pencil, that match the image in my head. (Figure 2) Next, I take a kneaded eraser and lightly erase over the entire drawing. The correct lines will usually stay in place because I drew them with the pencil point and not the side. (Figure 3) Finally, I finish the drawing by adding shading and finer details—because once the underlying structure is in place, it's fun to let loose and noodle away until the character is breathing. (Figure 4)

FIGURE 2

FIGURE 3

FIGURE 4

Remember, it's a process. Following grammar, logic, and rhetoric means starting with basic shapes, erasing the incorrect lines, then polishing it off with style!

To show the specifics, I have included staged drawings of six of my main characters: Tyrion, Jon, Dany, Arya, Cersei, and Robb.

TYRION

I love drawing Tyrion—and part of my inspiration for Tyrion is actually the Incredible Hulk. The character description portrays him as a monster—at least as far as looks go. So I gave him a big brow, big chin and jaw, and a short nose. I also had to keep the Lannister features in mind, to make sure he still looked related to his siblings. But to really sell Tyrion, he has to come off as smarter than everyone around him. So he usually has a smirk or an eyebrow raised. He always has something clicking in his mind. He is by far the most fun to draw.

JON

When drawing Jon (and indeed all of the characters), I was instructed *not* to be influenced by the actor or the TV show. Fair enough! My thinking was: How about a metal-loving high-school kid? I was in that group! While I didn't have long hair, I had plenty of friends who did. So eyebrows slightly raised in the "Not again . . ." expression and a drawn, sullen mouth. Jon always feels slightly outcast. He can hide behind his hair when he is emotional, just like the cowl of the Night's Watch. When angry, he'll drop his head and stare from under his brow. The books told us that Arya, Jon, and Eddard had similar features, and the other Stark kids favored Catelyn. So I gave Jon, Arya, and Eddard square button noses and square eyebrows.

DANY

Dany probably changes the most of any character. She was a tough one to figure out since we had to keep her age kind of ambiguous. We have laws, after all! It was also difficult to switch between Dany and Cersei. In the end, I settled on bigger eyes and dark eyebrows for Dany. Why dark eyebrows? *Not* because of the show! In comics, emotion is one of the most difficult things to draw. Most artists have four or five stock expressions. I challenged myself to have way more than that—and the decision came down to the fact that dark eyebrows emote better than white or blond. The thing that makes Dany unique is her growing self-confidence. So once her brother was toasted, I drew her head held high and her expression tilting toward the serious side. She is on a mission!.

ARYA

Arya is a fireball through and through. Some of the characters' personalities are initiated by an event, but I feel like Arya was born this way. She doesn't take any shit from anyone. The character descriptions portray her as almost ugly. Now, sometimes we make bad decisions as artists, and this was one of mine. I let my long-term outlook affect how I drew her because I didn't want to draw an ugly little girl for twenty-four issues. In hindsight, I regret it. A few issues in, I realized my mistake and suddenly had a problem to solve. My solution was to draw her angry and scowling and almost disheveled. As with Jon and Eddard, she has the trademark square nose. Arya's character, or essence, influences you when you draw her. Come at me, bro!.

CERSEI

The Lannisters are plentiful in *A Game of Thrones.* My take on them was to allow their house sigil of the lion to influence their looks. I made them all possess catlike features. They are sleek and regal, like runway models. Cersei is a sexy, conniving bitch; there is no other way to put it! I drew her with disgust, and it was *awesome*! I had fun with her clothing, too. To make her feel more powerful, I had her act with her hands as much as her face. She can control a room, no doubt about it.

ROBB

Robb is the flip side of the Jon and Arya Stark coin. He has his mother's features, like the rest of his siblings (save Arya and Jon). I gave them all triangular eyebrows and a swoopy tip to their noses. Halfway through *A Game of Thrones*, Robb grew a beard and began to reflect his father's presence. I feel that Robb wasn't quite a natural leader, but he had a strong will and worked hard. He grew into his role in his quest to avenge his father. While not as emo or brooding as Jon, Robb also carries his nostalgia for home on his sleeve.

And that concludes the process. I've had fun, and I hope you have, too. And if it's in your heart and soul to create, then by all means do it. Thanks!

GEORGE R. R. MARTIN is the #1 *New York Times* bestselling author of many novels, including the acclaimed series A Song of Ice and Fire—*A Game of Thrones, A Clash of Kings, A Storm of Swords, A Feast for Crows,* and *A Dance with Dragons* as well as *Tuf Voyaging, Fevre Dream, The Armageddon Rag, Dying of the Light, Windhaven* (with Lisa Tuttle), and *Dreamsongs Volumes I* and *II.* He is also the creator of *The Lands of Ice and Fire,* a collection of maps from A Song of Ice and Fire featuring original artwork from illustrator and cartographer Jonathan Roberts as well as *The World of Ice & Fire* (with Elio M. García, Jr., and Linda Antonsson). As a writer-producer, he has worked on *The Twilight Zone, Beauty and the Beast,* and various feature films and pilots that were never made. He lives with the lovely Parris in Santa Fe, New Mexico.

DANIEL ABRAHAM is the author of the critically acclaimed fantasy novels *The Long Price Quartet* and *The Dagger and The Coin.* He's been nominated for the Hugo, Nebula, and World Fantasy awards, and has won the International Horror Guild award. He also writes as M. L. N. Hanover and (with Ty Franck) as James S. A. Corey.

TOMMY PATTERSON'S illustrator credits include *Farscape* for Boom! Studios, the movie adaptation *The Warriors* for Dynamite Entertainment, and *Tales from Wonderland: The White Night, The Red Rose,* and *Stingers* for Zenescope Entertainment.